D0585530

A PLACE IN THE SUN

Recent Titles by Judith Saxton from Severn House

FALSE COLOURS
THE LOVE GIFT
THE SILKEN THREAD
WATERLOO SUNSET
THE WINYARD FORTUNE

A PLACE IN
THE SUN

Judith Saxton

severn
House

This title first published in Great Britain 2002 by
SEVERN HOUSE PUBLISHERS LTD of
9–15 High Street, Sutton, Surrey SM1 1DF,
complete with new Introduction from the author.
Originally published 1982 by Hamlyn Paperbacks
under the title *Flight to Happiness* and pseudonym *Jenny Felix*.
This title first published in the USA 2002 by
SEVERN HOUSE PUBLISHERS INC of
595 Madison Avenue, New York, N.Y. 10022.

British Library Cataloguing in Publication Data

Saxton, Judith, 1936-
    A place in the sun
    1. Love stories
    I. Title
    823.9'14 [F]

    ISBN 0-7278-5796-7

Printed and bound in Great Britain by
MPG Books Ltd., Bodmin, Cornwall.

For Elaine Richards,
There's many a true word…!

Introduction

I began writing this book because I had been invited to give talks on a cruise-liner sailing in the Caribbean; imagine a free holiday in a part of the world I had never expected to visit. So I began to read up on the area, and chose Barbados as a romantic and exciting setting.

Unfortunately, the book was the nearest I got to the island, as on sailing-day my husband Brian was in hospital, about to have his gall-bladder whipped out. So my "Place in the Sun" turned out to be North Wales in cold March weather. But that didn't stop Deborah from reaching Barbados – and finding romance there...

1

'So you're really going, I'll miss you of course, but I think you're doing the right thing, though you know what everyone'll say.'

Deborah Barnett, sitting in her friend Sally's plush office on the edge of the visitor's chair, nodded.

'Of course. They'll say I'm running away because Richard jilted me. Much I care what they say! And anyway, there's a grain of truth in it. I did find it difficult seeing him with Carlotta, at first. Not because I'd any feeling of affection or anything, but because Carlotta's such a bitch. I knew she'd flaunt Richard, wear him like a medal, and people would stare and whisper the way they stared and whispered over me. You know, the youngest, most go-ahead executive the firm's ever known, taking up with an eighteen-year-old typist . . . that kind of thing.' She grimaced. 'Hurt pride made me decide to leave, and now that I've landed such a dishy job I'm grateful to both of them. Truly!'

'Carlotta isn't eighteen. More like twenty-eight.' The girls grinned at each other. Sally picked up her typewriter cover and fitted it neatly over her machine. 'As for Richard, I think it just proved how shallow he really is. And to be blunt, Carlotta's only attraction is that she's anyone's. There! No one has to teach *me* how to cut up a character!'

'Nor me.' Deborah got up from her chair and began to file the letter-copies in Sally's out-tray. 'I know Carlotta's easy, and I'm the opposite, but I never thought Richard would expect me to "prove I cared" by sleeping with him.' She made a derisive noise and slammed the file drawer shut. 'The old "if you loved me you would" line absolutely sickens me, especially when it's trotted out after a mere four weeks of whirlwind courtship. And then he had the nerve to tell me all blondes are cold . . . well, for two pins I'd have treated him to some Latin temperament and done some face-slapping and back-stabbing, just to prove how extremely hot I felt.'

'Yes, I know, you wanted to dance on his hat and kick his cigar out of his mouth,' Sally said understandingly. 'It's a drag to be British, sometimes. Now that you've landed it, though, are you going to tell me about the new job?'

'Natch. Let's go to Ma Kettle's for pie and chips, and I'll give you the gen. I leave the country a week tomorrow, let me tell you!'

'Then it *is* abroad! I guessed it would be, when you got all mysterious about the job. What do your parents say?'

Deborah opened the door leading into the softly lit corridor and held it for her friend, then they both made their way to the cloakroom to fetch their outdoor things and titivate. The room was deserted, for most of the staff left on the dot of five o'clock and it was already twenty past. Deborah ran a comb through her thick, dark blonde hair and Sally, a striking brunette with a mannequin's walk and poise, put on a new layer of dark lipstick.

'My parents? I rang mother, and she said I might as well do as I pleased since I always had. And I rang father, only *she* answered the phone, so I just gave a message to say I was going away for a while and would forward my address. Lucky I *am* eighteen; they can't stop me even if they wanted to.'

'I take it *"she"* is his second wife? The one who brought you up after the split?'

Deborah nodded gloomily.

'If you can call it bringing up. Though, to be fair, a thirteen-year-old isn't the easiest proposition for a second wife to take on.'

Sally smoothed her hair and went over to the coat-rack, returning with a slim, dark violet coat with a pale fur collar, and a Robin Hood hat in the same dark violet, with a creamy plume which matched the collar. Deborah, bringing back her own rather shabby camelhair coat, immediately seized the hat.

'Gee whizz, is this the latest? Can I try it on?' She put it on her head, turned this way and that before the mirror, then pulled a face and handed it back to Sally. 'Sad, that. I adore hats and look a prune in them, and you manage to make them look even better on than off.'

'It cost the earth,' Sally said, placing the hat at just the right angle on her dark curls. 'You won't buy what suits you, you just buy the cheapest. And look, tonight's my treat, and we won't go to Ma Kettle's, we'll go to the San Marino. After all, you'll be lashing out all your savings on the plane ticket, I suppose.'

'A plane ticket to the Caribbean would cost the earth — I'm a kept woman, for the plane trip at any rate.' Deborah headed for the door. 'Come on, I adore Italian food.'

'The Caribbean?' Sally pressed the lift button and got in as the doors slid smoothly apart. 'Gosh, you lucky kid! I can't wait to hear about it. Have you brought some glorious summer outfits? You might have let me help!'

'I haven't bought anything yet. Remember, I'm a mere member of the typing pool, not a top secretary, like you,' Deborah said cheerfully as the lift hummed downwards. 'However, I'm getting all the money I paid into the pension fund back, and I'm going to get some dresses and a bikini with that. As I was coming back to the office I saw a marvellous lightweight suit, which might be just the thing; it was in a sale.'

'Coming back? Don't say you were running errands on your last day! Not for *Richard?*'

'Well, yes it was, actually.' Deborah flushed a little. 'He doesn't know I'm leaving, of course; I made the boss swear not to tell anyone. Anyway, Richard came up to my desk and put a tenner on it, and said would I go and get him some roses and some chocolates. He added, looking past my left shoulder all the while, that he was taking Carlotta to the ballet, so red roses would seem appropriate. I daresay he expected me to weep or ignore him, but I just said, "Certainly, sir," and went on typing. He looked quite taken aback.'

The lift reached the ground floor and the two girls began to cross the marble-floored foyer, heading for the revolving doors through which they could dimly see the dark dampness of the February day and the familiar, jostling commuters on the pavements, hurrying home.

'You don't bear a grudge, Debbie; in fact, you've got a lovely nature,' Sally said ruefully. 'Oh, it's raining, hold on a second whilst I get my umbrella ready.'

But Deborah, glancing back, suddenly plunged into the revolving doors, dragging Sally after her. Sally also glanced back.

'What's the matter? It was only Richard . . . I think he wants to speak to you.'

8

'I bet he does! Quick, into the underground!'

Urged on by Deborah's hand, Sally reluctantly descended the slippery steps into the tube station, jostled by men and women hurrying for their trains and having her hat knocked askew by a half-furled umbrella. Sally glared at the owner.

'Do you mind! This hat cost the earth.' Then, turning crossly to Deborah, 'Darling, let's get out of here. Richard won't pursue you down here, he's far too taxi-minded. Didn't you get his flowers and chocolates? I don't blame you a bit, but he wouldn't chase after you for that, he'd just get them himself!'

'I got them, all right. Put them on his desk, just as he asked me. Red roses.'

'So why the rush away from Richard?' Sally's hat was knocked by another elbow, and, exasperated, she made for the exit. 'Come on, let's get out of here before we're trampled to death! You can explain as we go why Richard seemed to put the fear of death into you.'

'The roses were lovely, done in a sort of heart shape,' Deborah explained breathlessly as they fought their way up to pavement level again. 'I got him a wreath, Sal. And the chocolates came from the chemist — half a dozen bars of that laxative. It cost every penny of the tenner.'

Sally stopped dead and gave a whoop of laughter, then, despite commuter glares, turned and hugged her friend.

'Oh, Debbie, I adore you! I'm going to miss you like hell! I wish I could have seen Richard's face when he saw the wreath.'

'That was why I came to your office early,' Deborah said frankly. 'I wanted to see his face all right, but I didn't want him to see mine. It's glorious, really, because of course he'll lie in wait tomorrow and I shan't turn up. He might even go round to the flat.'

'And you've given up the lease and moved into my spare room,' Sally said, staring at her friend. 'You don't really care about Richard, do you? No, I can see you don't; it was just your wicked sense of humour.'

'He reaped every one of those roses, and that chocolate,' Deborah said. 'It was nasty to pick me out of all the typists in the pool to get his damned flowers, and of course I showed the wreath round before I put it on his desk. He'll take a while to live it down.'

'Good. And once we're in the San Marino, sitting opposite the biggest helping of ravioli that money can buy, you can spill the beans about this job.'

*　　*　　*

'I saw this advert for someone who speaks good French to go to St Lanya, in the Caribbean, to look after a small boy. His father wants him to learn English — they're French — and since my French is good, I applied.'

'Your French must be good to be able to do short-hand in it,' Sally agreed. The two girls were sitting at a secluded table in the little Italian restaurant that Sally favoured, with the promised ravioli before them and a platter of crusty bread and dewy pats of butter to hand. 'In fact, I always knew you wouldn't stay with the company longer than a year or so. I just didn't expect you to go the way you did.'

Deborah giggled and buttered another piece of bread.

'Suddenly, you mean? It wasn't all that sudden,

really. I got an interview about three weeks ago, with the boy's grandmother; she's nice but severe. She conducted the interview in French and in English — her English is almost perfect — and then said that though I was rather young, I was easily the most suitable applicant, and would I care to accept such and such a salary? I agreed so quickly that she must have wondered if I was on the run from the police or something, but she took up my references and everything was all right, so here we are!'

'And what's the set-up? Will you teach English formally? Live with the family, or in lodgings, or what?'

'Heavens, Louis — that's the child's name — is only just five; they don't want him taught formally at all. They want me to look after him, speak English most of the time but French when he needs to be understood and can't manage it in English, I think. I'll live with the family, in a room which is either near or actually connected with the child's room. The grandmother, Madame Frenaye, couldn't tell me a lot, because she hasn't visited St Lanya much since the boy was born. But there's a beach, a boat, they've got a car . . . ' she beamed at her friend. 'I can't wait to get there, Sally!'

'Mm hmm. Why is English important, if they're French?'

'Oh, didn't I say the mother was English? She left her husband ages ago and Madame Frenaye said that the boy's been looked after by servants because her son was always off somewhere on business, but that they want him, eventually, to go to school in England, English education being the best in the world and all that. Madame said the boy needs a mother and a father, a stable background I suppose, but failing that, he should have someone young

11

enough to sympathise with his needs. Which is me.'

'Why doesn't he marry again, I wonder — Monsieur Frenaye, I mean,' Sally said, scraping her earthenware dish clean of the last delicious smear of ravioli. 'If his wife left him soon after the boy was born, you'd have thought he'd have found someone else by now.'

'Probably fat and hideous — rich men usually are — ' Deborah said, 'with halitosis and fallen arches and dandruff and . . . '

`Shut up, I'm still eating bread and butter! Is there no woman of the house?'

'I don't think so. A sister-in-law came to stay nearby, when Monsieur Frenaye returned to St Lanya, but Madame Frenaye didn't say whether she was still there.'

'Oh. Is she young, old? Didn't she say?'

'Well, I expect she's old; otherwise she could help with Louis,' Deborah said optimistically. 'Too old to interfere, I hope. If she's still in St Lanya, of course.'

'So the ménage consists of Papa Frenaye, Louis, you, and the servants. Blimey, servants, in this day and age! I bet Papa Frenaye's a stunner and you'll fall madly in love with him, and when you're married you can invite old Aunt Sally to stay. That is, if . . . Hooray, here comes our Partrina di Cappone Trevi, looking absolutely delicious, and I'm starving already!'

*   *   *

Deborah's pale grey suit with the dark red silk shirt beneath it had looked downright summery at Heathrow, and she had needed the thick camelhair coat over it. Here, in this brilliant sunshine with the sky and the sea such a deep, unreal blue and the palms

12

swaying above the white beach, the suit seemed too formal, and the coat downright ridiculous. By the time she had gone through customs, crossed the echoing hall and glanced at the people waiting behind the barrier, a light film of perspiration had broken out all over her and she knew she must shed the coat or die. The trouble was, she was so laden. She stood like a pack-pony in the thick coat, with a heavy suitcase weighing her down to the right and her overnight bag weighing her down a little less to the left. Around her neck her camera, a Biro on a necklace and her purse with her passport in it threatened to strangle her, whilst her handbag dangled limply from one wrist and her tennis racquet, complete with press, was propped up against her knee.

Nevertheless, if she was to survive, the coat must come off! She put the suitcase down, slid handbag and overnight bag on to the floor, and began to struggle out of the sleeves, having first undone the only button which remained done up. As she bent forward, her camera swung forward too and clunked against her suitcase. The tennis racquet clattered to the floor and Deborah swore beneath her breath. This was beginning to be irksome. She was bending over to retrieve the racquet when a voice spoke behind her. A deep, masculine voice, with a hint of amusement in its cadences.

'Keep still, mademoiselle, whilst I assist you.'

Hands eased her coat off, untangled straps, deftly caught a couple of magazines which she had shoved insecurely into her coat pockets. She glanced over her shoulder, knowing she must have looked a complete fool, and all but gasped. The handsomest man! Very tall, with thick, dark hair cut to show the shape of his head and light blue, very penetrating eyes. His mouth was amused, but she knew at once that she had scarcely registered with him. He had rescued her as an animal lover would fish an importunate kitten from a pond. His eyes roamed the people around her even as she stammered her thanks and began to reassemble her various property.

'You await someone, mademoiselle?' He smiled briefly when she nodded, then gave a small bow and moved away towards another group of incoming passengers.

For a moment, Deborah could only gaze after him. A Frenchman, and dishier than any man she had ever met before. Wouldn't it be funny, if . . . She dismissed the thought with an inward sigh. The man had known whom he wanted to meet, he had gone off with a purposeful step, and anyway, things like that happened in fiction and not in real life. Resolutely, she began to pick up her property. She had better make her way to the line of taxis and private cars outside the terminal buildings and see if anyone was waiting for her. Madame Frenaye had said she would be met, but arrangements could go wrong, particularly over such a distance. Fortunately, she knew the name of her employers and their address, so she could always get a taxi.

In the end, though, it took her two journeys to carry all her luggage out to the front of the building and once there, she hesitated after all to hail a taxi. It would look so rude to turn up there, only to find her employer missing, having gone to the airport to meet her. Anything might have happened; he might have been held up, or be sitting in one of the cars which were parked nearby, waiting to recognise her. Madame Frenaye would surely have given her son a description and there weren't that many blue-eyed blondes at the airport today!

People pressed past her, hailing taxis, getting into cars, or walking briskly off in the direction of the town. Poor Deborah saw the waiting vehicles dwindle down to one ancient hackney cab and glanced forlornly back at the airport buildings. Should she grab that taxi, or should she go back inside and ask someone if she might ring the Frenaye villa? Then, striding towards her, she saw her rescuer. He eyed her for a second, then came over to her.

'Excuse me, mademoiselle, I have to meet an English lady who was supposed to be on your flight; I wonder if you could . . .'

'Could it be me? I'm Deborah Barnett,' Deborah said without much hope. 'I'm waiting for a Monsieur Frenaye to . . .'

He had very thick, very black brows. First they rose almost to his hairline, then they descended in a heavy frown over his light eyes.

'*You* are Miss Barnett?' He made no attempt to hide either his astonishment or his disapproval. 'I gave my mother instructions to employ a woman of mature years, someone sensible, who could take full responsibility for a somewhat difficult child, not a . . . a . . . *jeune fille!*'

'I *am* sensible. I'm quite capable of looking after your son and,' Deborah switched to French, ' . . . I can speak your language every bit as well as you can speak mine! Damn it, what does age matter if my qualifications are right?'

He looked a little taken aback, then he shrugged — a very Gallic gesture — and held out his hand. Hesitantly, Deborah put hers in it.

'I'm sorry, Miss Barnett. I cannot blame you, I suppose, for my mother's mistake. And you may well prove every bit as sensible as you claim.' The light eyes, however, travelled cynically over her luggage and her somewhat warm and dishevelled person with a world of doubt in their depths. 'My car is over there — see the dark red sports model — so I'll drive you home and we can talk as we go.'

They reached the car and M. Frenaye opened the passenger door, then took her suitcase round to the boot.

'You get in, mademoiselle, whilst I put this away.'

Easier said than done! Deborah began to divest herself of her various impedimenta, unslinging her camera from around her neck, throwing her coat on to the back seat and her tennis racquet on top of that then, recklessly, her overnight bag on top of that.

She was still very hot, though, so began to divest herself of her thick grey jacket. Monsieur Frenaye, who had shut and locked the boot, came round and held the car door for her, his mouth set in a grim line as she struggled out of the tailored garment.

'I'm sorry, but I had to take it off,' Deborah said, completing her task and getting hastily into the front passenger seat. 'You've no idea how hot it is here.' One eyebrow jerked slightly. 'After London, I mean,' she added hastily.

He closed the door on her and walked round to his own side of the car, then slid behind the wheel.

'There's no desperate hurry.' He watched her struggle with the safety belt, then took it from her with barely restrained impatience and clipped it into the shank. He slid the car into gear, roared the engine, and they moved off, only to stop a few yards further on. Deborah, glancing enquiringly at him, saw he was eyeing her with exasperation.

'Do you want me to drive on, mademoiselle?'

What a sarcastic brute he is, Deborah thought crossly. She pitied his poor little son.

'Why not, monsieur?'

She spoke crisply, her words edged with annoyance.

'Because you put a red handbag down on the tarmac whilst you took off your jacket. I noticed it in the driving mirror as I pulled away and thought it possible that you wished to return for it, but if you'd prefer to leave it . . . '

Deborah, flushing every bit as red as the handbag, began to struggle with her safety belt release but suddenly, it seemed, he took pity on her, for he laughed, patted the hand that was fumbling with the belt, then left the car and fetched her bag, tossing it lightly on to the back seat before returning to his place behind the wheel.

'I'm sorry, Miss Barnett, that wasn't kind. You're hot and tired, and probably suffering from jet lag.' She glanced towards him, the blush slow to die, humiliation still making her lip tremble convulsively, but he was not looking at her. 'I'm afraid I came out of the house in a bad mood, which wasn't improved on learning that my mother had chosen to ignore my explicit instructions. I'll explain the situation as I drive. All right?'

'Of course. But explain what? Your mother merely said that your son wanted a nanny who would speak to him in English but who could speak French. Is there more to it than that?'

'A good deal, I'm afraid. My mother knows very little about Louis and our lives here. She disapproved of my marriage, and then disapproved of the fact that I made no attempt to remain with my son but paid servants to bring him up. As far as she knows, Louis is a nice, quiet little French boy who needs to learn English so that he can go to an English school, as I did.' He paused, then glanced over his shoulder, touched the indicator, and drew off the road into a shady lay-by beneath shaggy palm trees. 'I'm sorry, I find I can't drive and talk, we'll park here whilst I explain.'

He turned to face her, and Deborah realised why he had changed his mind about talking as they drove. He wanted to be able to gauge her reactions from her expression as the explanations were made. She kept her expression neutral, however, and raised her brows enquiringly.

'Well, Monsieur Frenaye? I do hope this isn't going to be a Jane Eyre situation.'

It surprised a crack of laughter out of him and brought an answering smile to Deborah's mouth. So he was human after all! The light eyes were frankly appraising her now, taking in the shining bell of her honey-coloured hair, the blue of her eyes, even the curve of her breasts beneath the thin silk shirt.

'No, mademoiselle, there's no mad wife, no sinister retainers, and my son is legitimate and not the offspring of an opera dancer. Though if you care to see me as Mr Rochester . . . ' a gleaming glance which brought the blood rushing to her face again. 'That seems to embarrass you; how the English do blush! No, the story, if such it can be called, is more commonplace. My wife left me when Louis was six months old and his nanny, Estelle Cranbarra, took over. She is fat, cuddly, and speaks a sort of French patois which she taught the boy. That, alas, is all she did teach him. Louis is five and cannot even tie his own shoelaces. Or rather, does not. He is intelligent, self-willed, and extremely obstinate. Over the past six months, since I came back here to live in fact, I've managed to get him to speak reasonably good French, but since he hardly ever addresses me, that does not mean much. My sister-in-law, knowing I'd made up my mind to return here permanently to bring up the boy, volunteered to come over here as well and help me with Louis.'

'Didn't it work out?'

'No. Renata doesn't speak French, which was a drawback, and though she's very capable and loves children, Louis took a dislike to her. His nanny, too, did not get on well with Renata and actually had to be dismissed because she was so obstructive. However, Estelle still lives on the Frèremaison estate and Louis is for ever running over to chatter to her, and becomes both emotional and aggressive when brought back.'

'Then does your sister-in-law live at Frèremaison too?'

'No, she's staying in an hotel and comes over two or three times a week. But if things work out and you manage to teach Louis manners as well as English things may . . . well, at least I'll be able to invite Renata to the house and know that she won't be insulted by Louis promptly quitting the place and rushing off to Estelle.'

'It's only natural that Louis should love the woman who brought him up, Monsieur Frenaye,' Deborah said mildly. 'He's only showing his loyalty, perhaps, and you can't expect to replace his nanny in his affections if he scarcely knows you.'

He glanced quizzically at her, a dark brow, rising.

'A practising child psychologist, I see! Of course he loves Estelle, but he should not love only her. He needs other company besides that of an ageing, bigoted old woman. Your job, Miss Barnett, will be to turn a young savage full of superstitious prejudice and unbridled temper into an ordinary little boy who I can safely despatch to a good English school. I hope, in short, that you will persuade him to put his love for Estelle into perspective. Important, yes. Deep, certainly. But not the be-all and end-all of life.'

'That seems sensible,' Deborah said cautiously. 'I see what you meant, monsieur, when you said that there was more to this job than your mother realised. Or perhaps she *did* realise. My own mother left my father when I was twelve, and a year later my father remarried. I disliked my stepmother only fractionally more than she disliked me, and her own children, all very young, became my responsibility. Oddly enough, I loved them dearly, and saw that in many ways the situation was a difficult one for them, too. They were three and five when my father married and brought us all to live together. Your mother drew all this information from me at the interview, and it may have occurred to her to set a thief to catch a thief.'

There was a pause during which he frowned at the palm trees at her back before he spoke.

'I understand you, I believe, but the two cases are not altogether similar. Renata loves children, and finds Louis charming. It is he who dislikes her.'

'That's just what my stepmother would have said if challenged,' Deborah assured him. 'I take it, then, that you are particularly anxious for Louis and his aunt to become good friends?'

'Well, it would ease matters.' He shot her a very straight look and his mouth quirked humorously. 'You are shrewd, mademoiselle. I begin to think that first impressions can be mistaken.'

'I quite agree,' Deborah said warmly. 'Why, when you came over and untangled me from my coat, I thought how charming you were!'

He gave her a quick glance, then smiled grimly.

'You are nobody's fool, Miss Barnett. I think you may well sort out our problems up at Frèremaison!'

2

Deborah woke next morning wondering where she was — for a moment, she almost wondered who she was — and then a movement in the doorway between her room and Louis's alerted her. Of course, she was on St Lanya and last night, briefly, she had been introduced to her charge who now stood staring at her apparently slumbering form.

Without moving, Deborah opened her eyes fractionally and studies the small, pyjama-clad figure through her lashes. Tousled, poised for flight, he was tip-toeing closer to get a good look and then, every bit as silently, he began to retreat.

Deborah waited until he was out of sight, then propped herself up on one elbow and shouted.

'Good morning, Louis!'

There was an audible gasp, followed by bedsprings pinging as a small weight abruptly landed on them. Deborah, wide awake now, slid out of bed and padded across the wood-block floor. Both rooms were whitewashed and airy, with wide windows and vividly patterned curtains and scatter rugs, but she had no time to waste now in admiring the interior of Frèremaison. Louis, sitting upright in his bed with eyes staring at her above the sheet, occupied all her thoughts. She crossed the room, smiling, and sat on the end of his bed.

'Well? Shall we get up and go exploring? Or do you prefer to lie in for a bit?'

She spoke in French, having decided last night that she must gain Louis's confidence before attempting to teach him anything. It had been obvious at once that Louis was sturdily determined to keep all his father's new friends at bay, and she was to be no exception!

'I do not mind.'

Leaning across, she pulled the sheet down, to reveal his small, freckled nose and a mouth set in a grim line. How like his father he looked, with the same thickly growing black hair, the same light blue eyes, and the same determined mouth and chin!

'Forgive my curiosity, Louis, I just wondered why you were holding the sheet over your mouth. I thought perhaps you'd taken your teeth out for the night, and felt shy that I might see you without them.'

Louis smiled reluctantly, showing small, pearly teeth.

'I do not take my teeth out. Do you, mademoiselle?'

'Only on special occasions. Shall we get dressed, then?'

'Why do you not take them out now?' Louis said, showing his teeth again in an appealing smile. 'Go on, mademoiselle!'

Laughing, Deborah shook her head.

'I was teasing, my little sausage! Shall we go and explore? Would you like that?'

He shrugged, feigning indifference, but she could see that she had caught his interest.

'I do not know where you would wish to go, mademoiselle.'

'Well, Louis, since I don't know Frèremaison, you

must be the leader. But I'd like to meet your nurse, Estelle, if you could take me to her. Your father tells me she's a very nice lady.'

A slight flush warmed his cheeks. He bounced once, then sat very still, his eyes on hers.

'Essie *is* nice, she would like to see you. She *said* she would like to see you. Some English ladies are not nice, but Essie might like you, perhaps.'

Deborah laughed. 'Right then, shall we go and see her after breakfast?'

'What's the time, mademoiselle?'

Deborah consulted her wristwatch, then gave a squeal.

'Gracious, Louis, it's only six o'clock; a bit early for calling on people! What time do you have breakfast? We could . . . '

Louis jumped out of bed and stripped off his striped pyjamas, casting them down on the floor.

'Essie gets up when the sun does, I often go and see her before breakfast.' He wriggled into a pair of scarlet shorts, then dragged a T-shirt, bright yellow with a rising sun on the chest, down over his head. He dragged on a well-worn pair of plimsolls, then eyed her expectantly. 'I'm ready. Bring your swimsuit and a towel; we could bathe.'

'Oh, but . . . ' Deborah felt that she should make some attempt to remind him of breakfast, his father's wishes, then pushed the words back, unsaid. If she was to gain this odd, attractive child's confidence, she must meet the woman who who had brought him up first. If Estelle was a bad influence on the boy then come what may, she would break the relationship. If not, then Estelle would be the greatest help in settling Louis down with his father and his new life. 'All right, Louis, I'll dress whilst you wash and clean your teeth.'

She guessed from the surprised look on his face that washing and cleaning his teeth had not occurred to him, but turned back into her own room.

'I will clean my teeth after breakfast, mademoiselle. And I will wash then, also.'

It was said challengingly, and Deborah accepted it as such. Friendship must not be gained at the expense of respect, not if she was ever going to be able to teach him anything. She turned in the doorway.

'It would be very rude to Estelle to go to her house dirty, with your teeth uncleaned. Do it now, please, Louis.'

There was a tense moment whilst he considered the matter, then he flashed her a smile and trotted over to the handbasin. As she slipped on a loose green sundress and pushed her feet into plaited sandals, she heard him begin to brush and could have sung aloud. First round to mademoiselle!

*   *   *

'There it is, mademoiselle, with the hens round the door. I'll give the cockerel a good kick if he comes at you, and then we'll be home!'

Deborah made no comment on Louis's choice of words, merely squeezed his hand. It was little better than a hovel, the cottage which crouched amidst the tropical palms and flowering shrubs, but it was more home to Louis than his splendid father's equally splendid villa!

'Here comes Prince Charles to say hello.' A villainous-looking mongrel dog came bouncing towards them. 'Don't be afraid, he's called Prince Charles because he's the nicest dog in the world and Essie says Prince Charles is the nicest man,' Louis explained. 'He never bites.'

Repressing a desire to reply that she was sure the dog's namesake was equally good with strangers, Deborah fondled the dog's soft, golden brown coat. Then she reached up and rapped on the front door, but before anyone could have opened it, Louis had bounced against it and hurtled into the room, crying, 'Essie, Essie, the English woman's come!' at the top of his voice.

'Come in, lady,' Essie Cranbarra said. She was a massive black woman, sitting in a rocking chair in the middle of her small and overcrowded living room. Deborah stepped forward, smiling, and took the chair indicated, glancing round as she did so at the brilliantly patterned curtains and cushions, the Welsh dresser laden with excellent but unmatched china, and the framed pictures of royalty which adorned the adobe walls.

'Good morning, Mrs Cranbarra,' she said cautiously. Essie beamed widely.

'You like a cuppa tea? I'm brewin'. So de lad brung you to see d'ole lady, eh? Early-early mornin' time, before dat Miz Brightmore gits to Frère-maison.'

Long ago, when Deborah had been very small, she had read and re-read a book called *Humpty Dumpty and the Princess*, and one of her favourite characters had been the Duchess. The Duchess was a golly with very long ears and she had heavy earrings hanging from the lobes. So did Estelle. The Duchess had curly grey hair and a mouth shaped like a pillar-box slit. So did Estelle. And from the Duchess emanated enormous strength of character and a good deal of warmth and charm. Snap, thought Deborah triumphantly. I liked the Duchess and I'm going to like Estelle!

'Yes, Louis brought me to see you, though I did ask him to. But couldn't I get the tea. You look nicely settled in that chair,' Deborah suggested.

'Dat's true, lady, though I *kin* move dis body, when I've a mind.' A broad, Duchess-like beam stretched the pillar-box mouth. 'Kettle's a-boilin', pot's stood ready. If you could jest stretch up and git another cup . . .'

'The work of a moment,' Deborah said, fetching a very beautiful, shallow blue and gold cup from the dresser. 'You've some lovely china, Mrs Cranbarra.'

'Dat's true.' An approving look. 'Long time since, when Monsieur Guy's parents live at Frèremaison, when de china him split and bust, dey give me good cups what's left. Yes, lady, all good stuff.'

Deborah, who guessed something of the sort by the variety of colours and patterns, nodded sagely.

'I daresay Monsieur Guy will do the same, now he's living here,' she said, pouring the tea. 'Sugar, Mrs Cranbarra?'

'I'se sweet enough.' A rich chuckle. 'And jest you call me Essie, lady, same's they all do. You met dat Miz Brightmore yet, lady?'

'Not yet. And if I'm to call you Essie, you must call me Deborah.' Deborah carried one cup to her hostess and took the other to her chair and sat down once more. 'I'm going to need your help to get Louis to settle down with his father up at the villa, and to allow me to teach him English.'

A gratified beam spread across Estelle's countenance. 'Dat suit me fine, Deb'rah. You welcome here any time, same's de boy.' She leaned sideways out of her chair. 'Hey, Louis, iffen you come here, speak me soft, mebbe I give you some gingerbread!'

Louis promptly appeared, carrying a struggling kitten by the neck in a stranglehold. Deborah jumped to her feet. 'Louis, that's the wrong way to hold a cat! Not round the neck; you must support his

26

little body, like this.' She took the kitten from him and demonstrated. 'See? Now the kitten likes being held, he won't fight or scratch.'

'What it matter, Deb'rah?' Essie was frowning. 'It only a kitten, dere plenty more. De boy like to squeeze . . .'

'It does matter, Essie. Suppose Louis had picked a baby out of its cot like that? He would treat any baby thing the same you know, even your grandchild! He could have dropped that baby on this hard floor, or stopped its breathing for long enough to kill it.'

'Hm.' The old woman frowned. She had been struck by the mention of a grandchild, Deborah could see that. 'Dessay you'm right, Deb'rah. How 'bout dat gingerbread?'

'I don't think so, thank you.' The old woman bristled and Louis's lower lip stuck out in a mutinous pout, but Deborah continued. 'We're going back to breakfast in a minute, M. Frenaye might be annoyed if Louis won't eat his breakfast because we've been here, eating gingerbread.'

'Who tell him?' the old lady enquired pugnaciously. 'Would you tell him, eh, lady?'

'Do you want Louis to learn that it's right to lie to his own father?'

Estelle stared at Deborah for a moment, then she began to shake. Her chins shook, her stomach, her ample bosom. Her cackle came next, and she mopped tears of mirth from her cheeks.

'You sho' know what you want, Deb'rah, and how to get it! You stan' up to ole Essie, I like that. And what's more, you'm right. We have gingerbread another day, hey?'

*   *   *

27

'You're late, Miss Barnett!'

Breakfast was served on the terrace, beneath a frangipani tree, for already it was warm enough to seek shade. Guy Frenaye sat on a white wicker chair, dark glasses hiding his eyes, a newspaper propped up against the coffee pot. He was wearing nothing but navy shorts and espadrilles and drops of moisture still clung to his dark hair.

'I'm sorry, monsieur.' Deborah, who had hurried back from Essie's house, envied him the bathe he had obviously just indulged in. 'Louis and I went visiting, and I'm afraid we forgot the time.'

'Visiting? You didn't . . . ,' he glanced down at Louis and gestured towards the open French windows leading into the dining room. 'Go and tell Suzannah you want your breakfast.' He turned to Deborah as the child disappeared and correctly interpreted her expression. 'Louis always eats in the kitchen, Miss Barnett. It is our mutual desire, not just my selfishness. Suzannah is a motherly soul who enjoys supervising his food. I dislike being forced to spend mealtimes either persuading Louis to eat or watching some of his more . . . unusual methods of devouring, say, spaghetti.'

Deborah's lips twitched, but she moved towards the French windows.

'I'd better eat in the kitchen too, then, since . . . '

'You'll eat here. Sit down!' He put out a foot and hooked another chair forward. 'Sit there, mademoiselle, and we can talk as you breakfast. At least it will enable us to discuss Louis's progress without the inhibition of his presence.'

Deborah sat stiffly on the edge of the chair and picked up the coffee pot, murmuring an apology as his newspaper fell on to the floor. Pouring the coffee, adding cream, she found that the beauty of the

28

morning, the sweetness of the air, did much to take the sting out of his high-handed attitude. He could have asked her to sit down instead of ordering her!

'Well? I take it you visited Essie?' ·

Deborah sipped her coffee sedately. It was delicious. She smiled demurely over her cup.

'We did.'

'Hm. Was that wise? Mrs Brightmore says Essie undermines my authority with the boy as soon as my back is turned.'

Deborah drained her cup before replying. Then did so calmly, seeing that her refusal to be flustered was annoying her employer for some reason.

'Essie's a sensible woman. If you ask for her co-operation I'm sure she'll give it willingly. She has fond memories of the days when your parents lived here.'

'Hm. Well, I don't want the boy down there every two minutes. That must be discouraged.'

Deborah put her cup back on the table and rose. Guy Frenaye rose also.

'Mademoiselle, our discussion is far from over. Kindly sit down again, and . . . '

'You must excuse me, monsieur. I'll just go along to the kitchen and see . . . '

He caught her arm in a grip which could not be denied and swung her round to face him. His eyes were very cold but his mouth was enjoying her furious attempts to escape. Furious and fruitless, for the more she tugged the tighter the fingers sank into the soft flesh of her upper arm.

'Let me go at once!' She spoke in furious English, her French momentarily forgotten. 'How dare you! Let me go!'

He held her still, smiling, breathing hard.

'When I've finished speaking, you may go where

you wish! Will you sit down quietly and listen, or must I continue to hold you?'

Disturbingly, Deborah was aware that his nearness was affecting her senses, that her dislike of being held between his hands was rapidly being overtaken by the pleasure of his nearness. Ridiculous, when he was nothing but a conceited bully!

'I'll sit down.' She sank into a chair and rubbed at the fingermarks printed on her upper arms. 'Another time, monsieur, try asking politely. You'll find I'm always happy to do as I'm asked if I can.'

'I see.' He smiled sardonically. 'Then please listen for a moment, mademoiselle, whilst I explain what plans I have for you and Louis.'

The colour was fading from her face and her breathing was steadying. She inclined her head graciously. 'Certainly, monsieur.'

'Good. In the mornings, immediately after breakfast you should try to teach Louis some simple English, or perhaps some English games, rhymes. Then, at eleven o'clock, I think you should repair to the beach, where you can swim together. Lunch is served at twelve-thirty and after that you will be free to do as you please until it is Louis's bedtime, at six o'clock. From six-thirty, when you leave him for the night, your time is once more your own. Is that clear?'

'Well, yes, but who will take care of him in the afternoons? If he's left to his own devices I expect he'll return to Essie.'

Monsieur Frenaye had been standing before her; now he turned to survey the glorious formal gardens which sloped down to the narrow roadway and, beyond that, the glittering blue of the sea. He answered with his head turned away.

'In the afternoons? My sister-in-law plans to take him for excursions, to places of interest. It seems

30

possible that this might prove a good way of winning his affection.'

'I see. And will you accompany them?'

He turned to face her again. 'Sometimes. When I'm not busy. But the afternoons will be yours to enjoy as you please. There is public transport into town from the top road; you can go out in the boat if you know how to use one, and I'm sure you'll soon make friends.' He came over to her and held out a hand. 'And now, mademoiselle, if you've really finished breakfast after one cup of coffee, I would be obliged if you would come swimming with me.'

'With you? But what about Louis?'

He eyed her quizzically.

'Louis shall come too, and play on the beach. The thing is, Miss Barnett, that I am going to leave my son to your care on an island surrounded by water. I want to make sure that you are a strong enough swimmer for such a charge.'

'Oh.' It seemed fair enough. 'Very well, I'll go and change into my costume.'

He nodded glancing at his heavy gold wristwatch.

'Good. I'll see you on the beach in twenty minutes.'

*　　*　　*

'Come along, Miss Barnett, the water isn't cold, you know!'

Deborah, in a pale yellow swimsuit, dabbled her toes uncertainly in the creaming surf. She *could* swim — just — but it had been four or five years since she had last done so, and the thought of looking a fool before Monsieur Frenaye was not appealing. He was in silver-grey swimming trunks, what was more, which showed off the tanned and muscular strength

31

of him, and made Deborah feel like an uncooked biscuit, all pale and wishy-washy.

'Miss Barnett, am I going to have to carry you in?'

The threat, uttered with a gleaming glance which told her how much he would enjoy carrying out the threat, galvanised her into action. Oh yes, he'd carry her in with the greatest of pleasure, she had no doubt of that. And drop her in out of her depth with even greater pleasure!

'I'm coming!' She set off splashily at a good speed, which gradually slowed as the water deepened. When it was up to her ribs, she took a deep breath, cast a scared glance at the man standing watching her sardonically, and launched herself into a prim and rather splashy breast stroke. She managed four feet or so before something touched her leg, brushing against it with enough force to make her shriek.

'Oh! Oh! Shark!'

The 'shark' surfaced beside her, grinning exactly like a shark, she thought crossly.

'No, mademoiselle, it was I, diving beneath you. Here, let me hold your chin, and you must put more strength into your strokes, more power.'

He held her chin and she panicked, lashing out wildly; then felt his arm encircle her waist, take in her weight effortlessly.

'Keep *still*, mademoiselle, I shan't let you drown! Now, slowly, slowly, move the arms, turn the head to one side . . . Don't breathe when your mouth is below the water, little goose, or you will assuredly drown!'

He was a good teacher, she had to admit that. After twenty embarrassing minutes he stood her down, held her shoulders, and smiled at her.

'Well, already you're managing a good deal better, are you not?' She looked up at him, nodding, her long hair in blonde mermaid tresses, her blue eyes only just blinked free of salt-water. She saw his face change, alter subtly, and then he had pulled her close to him, and his mouth sought hers, urgently, demandingly, in a kiss the like of which she had never known before so that blood surged to her face and her heart hammered in her breast, making her breath short, making her lean against him, making her . . .

'Guy! Hey, Guy, I'm back! The boy's gone rushing off somewhere . . . *Do* come out of the water and tell me what's happening!'

He released her so abruptly that she half fell, and had to be dragged upright again by hands that were indifferent, now, to her, for Monsieur Frenaye's eyes were focussed on the beach, and on the woman who stood there, calling out to him.

A tall woman, and slim, in a white dress with a gold tie-belt. Long, dark-red hair, green eyes, a pouting, sensual mouth. But Monsieur Frenaye was making for the beach, pushing his thick, dark hair back with both hands, calling out to the woman.

'My dear Renata, I didn't realise you were coming here this morning or I wouldn't have bathed so early. Are you coming in for a dip, or did you just come to see Louis?'

The woman flung back her head and laughed. She was tanned to a glorious shade of pale, creamy golden brown, Deborah saw enviously.

'Darling, as if I would! I've come to persuade you to take me shopping in Castlebridge for something special to wear to the De Roche's barbecue party.' Monsieur Frenaye was out of the sea now and turned, as if he had only just remembered Deborah. 'Who's your friend, Guy? You must introduce us.'

'I'm sorry. Miss Deborah Barnett, this is my sister-in-law, Renata Brightmore. Miss Barnett has

33

come to teach Louis both English and good manners,
I trust.'

Renata Brightmore held out a beautifully
manicured hand whose nails dripped scarlet and
Deborah put her own cold fingers into it. Renata's
handshake was a touch, no more.

'My successor, in fact!' She smiled brightly at
Deborah. 'I'm afraid I failed lamentably to get the
little boy's attention long enough to teach him anything. However, once he can speak some English I
hope we'll be friends.' She turned back to Guy.
'Come along, darling, and if you can get changed in
ten seconds flat we'll lunch at that marvellous seafood place. Does it appeal?'

He picked up his towel and hung it round his neck,
then turned carelessly to Deborah.

'I daresay you'll find Louis with Essie, Miss
Barnett. Bring him home for luncheon, won't you?
He usually rests after the meal for an hour. I'm afraid
plans for this afternoon are rather disarranged, but
you won't mind that.' He watched as she picked up
her towel and slung it round her own shoulders and a
shade of disquiet crossed his face. 'You've got very
white, very tender skin, so don't go lying about in the
sun, do you understand? Get back indoors and
change into a dress, and then tomorrow, after
luncheon, I'll run you into Castlebridge and we'll get
some lotion, so that you can tan without burning.'

Deborah muttered some conventional remarks
and waited until they had left the beach; then she
made her way slowly back to the villa. What a beastly
woman Renata Brightmore was! And as for
Monsieur Frenaye . . . but her mind sheered away
from that moment in the water when he had kissed
her, held her so demandingly close. It had been a
momentary whim for him, and no more than an

incident for her. Goodness knows, she had been kissed by enough men before, and it hadn't caused her heart to leap about in an undisciplined fashion. Think of the unlamented Richard! Think of Teddy Taylor in Accounts, who was thought to be quite a dish! Think of . . . But he was a Frenchman, that must be it, and they had kissed in a warm, tropical sea, with the sun blazing down and the water surging around them. Yes, that was it.

She crossed the hall, leaving a trail of damp, sandy footprints, and went up the stairs; then locked herself in the shower and turned the tap on cold. She would wash, not only the salt water but the memory of that kiss, right out of her mind!

3

Contrary to her expectations, however, Deborah saw nothing of her employer for the next week. It was the season, Suzanne informed her, when the sugar growers met to discuss their prices and plan their strategy for the market place. Monsieur Frenaye, Suzanne said proudly, did not merely own plantations on this island but had property elsewhere in the Caribbean as well. The estates were run in his absence by managers, to be sure, but they too had to be consulted before he could make up his mind how to plan his deals.

'You make it sound like a war,' Deborah said, and Suzanne, twinkling at her, said that perhaps it was a little like that. 'Did monsieur leave any instructions as to what I was to do in his absence?'

Suzanne shrugged.

'Madame Brightmore will be coming each day, will she not? Doubtless he has left instructions with her.'

There was that in Suzanne's tone which led Deborah to believe that Renata was not much loved by the servants, and the impression was strengthened by the smiling faces in the kitchen when, at the end of the week, she remarked to Suzanne and her helpers — little Poppy, who was maid of all work, and the chauffeur-handyman's wife, Doris — that something must be wrong with Mrs Brightmore.

'Maybe.' Suzanne was shelling peas with machine-like efficiency. 'Or maybe she just don't want to come up here when Monsieur Guy's away.'

'Well, whatever the reason, it's putting me in a difficult position,' Deborah said worriedly. 'We made definite arrangements about what time I could have off and so on, but Monsieur Frenaye made it plain that when I was out, Mrs Brightmore would be here. I suppose you don't know when he's coming back?'

Three heads shook.

'Well, I hope it won't be much longer. I suppose I could get in touch with Mrs Brightmore. But it seems odd, Suzanne, because monsieur saw me the day before he left and didn't even mention that he might be away.'

'No, he wouldn't have, because he didn't know,' Suzanne said, placidly hulling peas. 'He arranged for some young man from his Paris office to take over the work this year, thought it would be good experience for him, only the young fellow was taken ill the night you arrived. Monsieur rushed off in a temper, expecting to be back within a few hours, and found that his employee was too sick even to assist him. So he flew off to Jamaica. Why don't you go down to the estate office and talk to Tom Saunders? He'll know better than us when Monsieur Guy's likely to come back.'

'If you want to go shoppin', I'll take care of Louis, miss,' Poppy said shyly. 'We gets on well, Louis and me.'

'That's awfully kind of you, Poppy. But it isn't that so much.' Deborah looked round at their concerned faces. 'The truth is, I'm a bit short of money, so there isn't much shopping that I can do, and of course I don't know a soul, so I don't want to go gadding around the island. It just seems so strange that Monsieur Frenaye should go away and leave me, a comparative stranger, with his son.'

'We're here,' Suzanne remarked, beaming kindly at Deborah. 'We'd soon shout if you acted unfriendly to our Louis!'

'Yes, I suppose that's true. And he may have forgotten to remind Mrs Brightmore to come each afternoon, and have forgotten that he's forgotten. If you see what I mean!'

Poppy plainly did not, but the two older women nodded sagely.

'Easily done. Monsieur Guy's always busy,' Doris agreed. ' 'Sides, you and Louis are gettin' on fine.'

'That's true. In a way, Monsieur Frenaye couldn't have found a better way to start our relationship off, with the two of us thrown into each other's company from morning until night.' She turned as a small figure appeared in the kitchen doorway. 'Hello, darling, have you drawn that picture?'

Louis nodded and came right into the room, holding out a sheet of pale yellow sugar paper on which were chalked a number of strange symbols and signs.

'Yes. It looks like, doesn't it?' He held the paper up, peering at them over the top. 'Is it time for elevenses?'

'I'll put the kettle on presently,' Suzanne said, unzipping another pea pod. 'What would you like with your milk? Some biscuits, or a slice of fruit cake? Or there are doughnuts.'

'I'll have all of them.'

Suzanne beamed, but Deborah cut in quickly.

'What about a please, young man?'

Louis sighed.

'All of them please, Suzanne.'

'That means, I'll have whichever of the three you

think best, please, Suzanne,' Deborah interpreted. Louis stared at her.

'No, mademoiselle, it means I will have biscuits and fruit cake and doughnuts.' There was a pause. 'Oh! If you please!'

'Beautifully said, mon petit, but I'm afraid it's out of the question. You were given a choice, from which you must choose one.'

'Biscuits. No, a big piece of cake.' Louis said quickly, deciding to make the best of a bad job. 'Can I have it on the terrace, with mademoiselle? And can I have some coffee in my milk?'

'Louis, you're incorrigible,' Deborah sighed. 'You missed out three pleases. Don't forget the bad mark game!'

The three women turned enquiringly towards Louis, who smiled condescendingly.

'Do you not know the bad mark game, ladies?' he enquired. 'I, also, knew it not until a few days ago. It is *great* fun. For all the little goodnesses one performs, one gets good marks, and for the badnesses, bad ones. Then, at the end of the day, one counts up one's marks, and if one has more bad marks than good, there is no story, or no bedtime biscuit, or something of that nature. If one has more good than bad marks, however, one gets a treat!'

'I bring up your biscuits each night, and mademoiselle is always reading or telling a story,' Poppy objected. 'Never yet have you missed your biscuits!'

Louis smiled.

'Of course not. Always I get more good marks than bad. Where is my fruit cake?' He saw the looks on the faces of his audience and jumped visibly. 'Please, where is my fruit cake, please, Suzanne!'

Deborah laughed and kissed the top of his head,

then went into the pantry and came back with the cake tin.

'You don't mind, Suzanne? He's such a little gentleman — when he remembers!'

Later, sipping her own coffee on the terrace and watching as Louis dealt with the enormous slab of cake, she remembered Suzanne's remark about the estate office.

'Louis, darling, do you know your way to the estate office?'

He gulped his milk, put his mug down with a clatter, and wiped a milky moustache off his upper lip.

'Of course, mademoiselle. Shall we go there this morning? We could say bonjour to Essie and Prince Charles on the way.' He eyed Deborah hopefully. 'I'm teaching Prince Charles to beg. Do you think, perhaps . . . ?'

'I daresay Suzanne will give us some scraps. What was the name of that man Suzanne said I should see?'

Louis darted across the terrace, but turned in the doorway.

'Was it Monsieur Tom, perhaps? I'll ask Suzanne, shall I, when I get the scraps for Prince Charles?'

'Please, mon brave. It's not far, is it? To the estate office, I mean.'

'No, not far.' Louis's tone was vague. 'I wonder if Suzanne would like to give Prince Charles a dough-nut?'

* * *

In the event, the walk to the estate office turned out to be further than Louis had remembered, particularly, as he ingenuously informed her, since he had previously visited Mr Saunders by car.

However, the walk was beguiled by the presence of Prince Charles, lent for the occasion by a smiling Essie, who had been delighted that Deborah was about to meet someone other than the occupants of Frèremaison.

'Mr Saunders nice young fella,' she observed. 'He show you around, mebbe tek you to parties.' The smile vanished. 'Like Monsieur Frenaye should do,' she finished severely.

Now, strolling along the narrow tarmac road, with sugar canes rustling on one side of her and palms on the other, Deborah had leisure to consider the past week.

As she had intimated to the servants, she and Louis were getting along very well. As she had half-suspected, the little boy knew a lot more English than he had admitted, and with games, songs and poems to help him, he had already shown more fluency than anyone had expected. Even now, chasing Prince Charles who was in hot pursuit of a great tropical butterfly, Louis was singing in English, a song with a catchy tune and simple words concerning the whereabouts of a baby's dimple. Louis loved it. 'On the baby's knuckle, on the baby's knee, where will the baby's dimple be?' he carolled, and Deborah smiled with satisfaction. Monsieur Frenaye should be delighted with his son's progress when he returned home.

In a way, she supposed that it did not particularly matter that her employer was not actually at Frèremaison, since she knew no one, had no money for shopping, and was enjoying a very pleasant existence. But the responsibility for the boy, and even in a way for the house, weighed on her. If he had only warned her she would be in charge for a week! And then there was the sun oil. A small enough item to be sure, but she was so fair that even ten minutes of sun bathing flushed her skin uncomfortably, and unless she had some idea of the price of public transport she was unwilling to take herself and Louis off into town to buy sun oil which might turn out to be way beyond her means. If only she had not spent so much in London before leaving! If only she had resisted the lure of duty-free perfume on the aircraft! She sighed. It was no use wishing; she would just have to find out when Monsieur Frenaye was comming back, and hope that it would be soon.

The estate office proved to be a collection of sturdy wooden buildings set in a wide clearing in the forest. They were backed and shaded by palms, and roofed with shingle tiles, not with the corrugated iron which Deborah had noticed on some of the poorer dwellings as she had come from the airport.

'Where do we go to find Mr Saunders?' Deborah asked her small guide. 'Can you remember?'

'Of course.' Louis went straight to the door of the largest building and, disdaining knocks, flung it open and marched inside. Over his shoulder he invited Deborah to follow him, then padded across to the reception desk which faced the door. 'Good morning, Barbara. This is my new English mademoiselle!'

The girl laughed, and Deborah found herself facing a large desk with several different coloured telephones on it, and a slim, dark girl who suspended her rapid typing to greet them. She held out a hand, which Deborah took.

'You must be Miss Barnett; I'm Barbara Franklyn. Can I help you?'

'I rather hoped I might see Mr Saunders, just for a moment. Is he in this morning?'

'Yes, he is. I'll ring through.' She picked up one of the telephones and pressed a buzzer, then said into the mouthpiece, 'Mr Saunders, there's a Miss Deborah Barnett from the house to see you.'

'Fine. Give me two minutes.'

It had been impossible not to overhear, so Deborah glanced round. There were comfortable cane chairs against the outer wall and the long windows, shielded with blinds, were open to let in what breeze there was. She held out a hand to Louis.

'Shall we sit down for a moment, Louis, just until Mr Saunders can see us?'

Prince Charles, who had accompanied them into the reception area, was taking far too keen an interest, Deborah thought apprehensively, in a huge rubber plant, so she was not displeased when Louis shook his head.

'I think, mademoiselle, that Prince Charles and I will go and see a friend of mine next door. Is that all right?'

Deborah was about to agree with the suggestion when one of the inner doors opened and a man in working overalls came out, followed by another, younger man. He was clad in an open-necked white shirt and drill shorts, his light brown curly hair stood on end, and he had a cup of tea or coffee in one hand, but Deborah knew at once that this was Tom Saunders, Monsieur Frenaye's estate manager. Despite the casual dress and his youth, an air of undoubted authority hung about him.

'Miss Barnett? Do come in, I'm sorry to be caught drinking coffee, but Barbara will make you a cup and we can take a break together.' He stood aside to let her into his office, and rumpled Louis's head. 'Hello, young man, long time no see. And Prince Charles, by all that's wonderful! Will he come in as well, or does he intend to inhale Barbara's rubber plant whilst we conduct our business?'

'I think perhaps Prince Charles would be happier out of doors,' Barbara said apprehensively. 'Here, boy!' They watched Prince Charles stroll out into the sunshine, then went into Tom Saunders' office and shut the door on the sound of Barbara making coffee.

'This is my new English mademoiselle, Tom,' Louis said importantly as soon as they had settled themselves, Deborah on one side of the desk, the estate manager on the other, and Louis leaning against the chair. 'We like her very much; don't you think she's pretty?'

'Very pretty,' Tom Saunders said, over Deborah's murmur of protest. 'You must learn, Miss Barnett, to accept a Frenchman's compliments with aplomb, especially since Louis is no Anglophile as a rule.'

'Yes, it was charming,' Deborah agreed. 'I'm sorry to cast myself on your mercy without so much as an introduction, Mr Saunders, but I really am rather worried about Monsieur Frenaye.'

'Tom, please. And may I call you Deborah?'

'Of course. How did you know . . . ?'

'That your name was Deborah? News travels fast on St Lanya, and even faster on the Frèremaison estate. From the moment you stepped into Essie's cottage and made it plain that you liked her, I dare-say half the island were prepared to befriend you. So it's a pity you've kept yourself hidden away, really.'

'I haven't hidden myself away.' Deborah looked earnestly across at him. He must be twenty-four or twenty-five, no more, and he was nice-looking, with deeply tanned skin and very shrewd grey eyes. She decided that she would confide in him, though she had, for some reason, expected him to be older, more fatherly. 'You see, Monsieur Frenaye was called away unexpectedly and since then I've not liked to go too far away from the house or to leave Louis in case instructions arrived for me, but the situation is rapidly becoming impossible. I need various things from the shops, but I haven't gone into town because, well . . . '

Her voice petered out. How could she explain, even to this nice young man, that she was almost penniless, had been relying on the prompt payment of her salary to buy postage stamps even? But Tom Saunders was no fool and guessed the rest from her pink cheeks and the way her eyes avoided his.

'Ah, if you want to go shopping, you'll need your salary, of course,' he said briskly. 'It really isn't like Monsieur Frenaye to neglect to make arrangements, but I'm afraid on this occasion things seem to have gone awry. I thought he said his sister-in-law would be visiting the house daily and would take care of things there, otherwise I would have either phoned or called, but I must have been mistaken.'

'No, I think Mrs Brightmore did intend to call, or so Monsieur Frenaye told me,' Deborah said. 'Unfortunately, however, Mrs Brightmore has neither called nor phoned, so I've been rather hamstrung. It wasn't until today, in fact, when Suzanne mentioned your name, that I knew you existed.'

'That's a body blow!' He grinned at her. 'Never mind, we can soon remedy that. I take it that Monsieur Frenaye gave you no idea when he would be returning?'

'No. He didn't know he was leaving, did he?'

'No, of course, I was forgetting that this year young Claude Durat was supposed to deal with the business. Well, look. Monsieur Frenaye spoke to me on the phone last night and said the work was all but finished, so he may well be back within the next couple of days.' Tom opened the top drawer of his desk and drew out a packet of biscuits, which he threw to Louis. 'Hey, Louis, did you know Eggy's got a new parrot? Sacré bleu, but you shouldn't miss seeing it! And it speaks for biscuits.'

'Oh!' Louis cast a longing glance at Deborah. 'May I go, mademoiselle? Just for a minute?'

'Of course, darling, but don't be too long.'

The door closed behind Louis and Tom leaned forward and passed an envelope across the desk. 'I've put thirty quid in there, just to tide you over until Monseur Frenaye returns. Then I'm sure he'll get your salary sorted out and it will go through with the rest of the wages, on a Thursday. And look, about this shopping; I'm going into town this afternoon and I'll happily give you and Louis a lift if that'll help.'

'It would be wonderful,' Deborah said frankly. 'But won't Louis be bored to tears? Kids usually hate shopping.'

'Not Louis; he so rarely gets taken into town that the novelty will keep him happy for an afternoon. He gets on well with me, too, so if you want to pop into a shop and browse, Louis and I can amuse ourselves for half an hour or so.'

'Oh, but you don't want to trail round after me! Haven't you business to attend to in Castlebridge? I can manage Louis.'

'No, not business exactly. I thought I might have a look at shirts, though. Honestly, I'd be happy to show you round.'

'Well, if you're sure . . . ' Deborah's thanks were interrupted by the abrupt arrival in the room once more of Louis, either being towed by Prince Charles or pushing him through the door ahead of him, it was difficult to see which. Louis was panting and looked distraught.

'Oh, mademoiselle, Prince Charles ought to have a bad mark. Poor Eggy's parrot!'

'Gracious, I never thought! Not . . . not *dead*, Louis darling?'

'Oh, no, mademoiselle. Just a little balded in the tail,' Louis confessed. 'But very *very* angry, mademoiselle. He called Prince Charles evil names, and said words which Eggy says I am never *never* to repeat!'

'In that case, I won't ask.' Deborah caught Tom Saunders' amused glance and smiled at him. 'I daresay it could have been worse; Prince Charles is . . . ' she saw Louis's eyes grow anxious ' . . . is so full of life,' she ended tamely.

'Eggy didn't think so. He said Prince Charles was a vicious pig,' Louis contributed. 'He said he would strangle Prince Charles with his bare hands if he ever came here again.' He tugged anxiously at Deborah's hand. 'Mademoiselle, shall we go home now, and have our lunch?'

'Don't worry, Louis,' Tom said as they crossed the reception hall. 'Eggy didn't mean it, he was just upset for his parrot. Eggy wouldn't hurt any bird or animal, you know that!'

'I'm sure that's true, but I think Louis is right and we'd better be getting back now,' Deborah said cheerfully. 'Goodbye, Barbara. Goodbye, Tom. We'll see you about two, and thanks very much for solving my problems.'

The two of them and the dog walked home contentedly, Louis delighted at the proposed visit to Castlebridge.

'There is an animal market,' he told her eagerly. 'Every animal can be seen there, puppies, kittens, monkeys, guinea pigs. Even parrots!'

'We'll look, certainly, but I daresay your papa would prefer to be consulted before we thought about buying anything,' Deborah said. Louis, however, was unperturbed.

'Oh, I know I may not have a pet, mademoiselle, or not just yet. One day, perhaps, when I'm bigger. But to see them, to stroke them, perhaps.' He heaved an ecstatic sigh. 'That is such fun!'

I really ought to talk to his father about his meeting other children, Deborah thought. He idolises Prince Charles and Essie, but when you think about it, he hasn't even one child anywhere near his own age to play with. I'll consult Monsieur Frenaye as soon as he returns.

*　　*　　*

'Well, Deborah, where shall we go first?'

They were standing by the harbour, surrounded by flamboyant and exciting little shops, with street vendors down by the quay like brightly plumaged birds, their wares spread enticingly out before them. Deborah smiled up at her companion and squeezed Louis's small hand.

'Tom, I'm intrigued by everything and completely lost, and Louis isn't much better. Just take us where we can find pretty clothes and then an icecream or two.'

'Right. We'll go to Thirsk's.'

Thirsk's proved to be a department store and it yielded a yellow satin bikini which Deborah could not resist and an apricot gold sundress which would be cool and easy to wear. But it was not at Thirsk's that Deborah found her dream dress. That was in one of the tiny, expensive boutiques surrounding the harbour. It was in the window, and was deceptively simple, just a swirl of white chiffon over a satin slip, but it was priced far beyond Deborah's means.

'Oh, Tom, look at that fabulous dress!'

Tom looked, then caught sight of the price ticket.

49

'Lumme, fabulous is the word! What's it made of? Gold dust?'

'Yes, I know, it's miles beyond my reach, really. Oh well, I've got the apricot silk one. Not that it's really silk, but it looks it.'

'Well, what about that deep blue one?' Tom suggested. 'It's awfully pretty, and about a tenth of the price.'

'Yes, but I've spent enough money on clothes for one day,' Deborah said, turning away from the shop window. 'I think it's time we put temptation out of sight and went and visited the animal market.'

Louis skipped and turned a beaming face up to hers.

'Oh, mademoiselle! Do you know, I like it best when papa's not here? We have fun, and there is no Aunt, and we even have an outing to my favourite place!'

'How about an icecream first, old boy?' Tom suggested hopefully. 'After all, the animal market is in the old town, where the heat will be greater, but we can cross the quayside and go straight into the Swiss Cottage and be feasting in two minutes! And resting our poor feet,' he added in an aside to Deborah.

Louis was agreeable, so Tom led them to what looked like a Swiss chalet on a holiday postcard, overlooking the harbour. They went inside, and found that the place was open to the sea breeze on one side, and that it was cool and dim, with small tables set at discreet distances from each other and waitresses in black frocks and frilly white aprons hurrying back and forth.

'It's an odd place, but wildly popular with the elite of St Lanya,' Tom said when he had ordered a dish of multi-flavoured icecream for Louis and tea and cakes for Deborah and himself. 'If you look round, you'll

50

probably see a lot of very expensive faces and dresses.'

Deborah looked round, then looked back again quickly as a familiar voice was raised at a table nearby.

'Desmond, darling, I simply *dare* not! It's all very well to talk of my perfect figure, but how do you think I keep it this way? Not by eating cream cakes, I can assure you.'

Her quick glance had already assured Deborah that it was Renata Brightmore, sitting with a short, thickset man in a white silk suit with a yachting cap pushed to the back of his greying hair, but at the sound of that voice she saw Louis stiffen, then push a spoonful of icecream into his mouth whilst swivelling his eyes round towards the voice.

'Oh, damn,' Tom muttered, following the child's glance. 'I should have guessed she'd be here! Not that it matters, but we don't want anyone to be put off their tea because of it.'

But Louis had obviously decided to ignore his aunt's presence. He sat back in his chair and looked out of the harbour, feeding himself with icecream every now and then and playing a game of 'Simon says' beneath his breath.

'Simon says touch your knee . . . ' suiting actions to words. 'Simon says wiggle your nose. Simon says give a lickle clap. Now touch your toes!' A triumphant stillness followed the last command.

The waitress, arriving with the tea and an enormous plate of cakes, took their minds off their company for a while and Deborah, pouring the tea into long glasses and adding the thin slices of lemon, was beginning to hope they might remain quietly unnoticed. After all, she reasoned, Renata only met me once, and that briefly on the beach, and she doesn't like children, so she probably won't glance across at Louis. We may well be all right.

She had reckoned without Tom's undoubted attractions.

'If we're going to meet for cocktails before the dance I'd better be getting back to the hotel,' the light, carrying voice remarked presently. There was a scraping back of chairs, then sounds of departure and then, when Deborah was beginning to relax, an exclamation, followed by the rapid tap of high heels on polished boards.

'Desmond, it's Tom Saunders, Guy's right-hand man!' Tensing, Deborah heard Renata come to a halt just behind her chair. 'Tom, darling, it's been *ages* since we met! Do intro — Oh!'

'Hello, Mrs Brightmore,' Deborah said, getting to her feet. 'It's only me and Louis. Tom was kind enough to bring us into town to do some shopping. And to give us tea, as you can see.'

Louis, his mouth smothered in icecream, kept his dark eyes fixed on his plate but his sandalled feet shuffled uncomfortably.

'Good gracious, is that my Louis?' Renata turned to her escort. 'This is my nephew, Desmond, the one I take out in the afternoons. Well, when I've time I do. You know, Guy Frenaye's son.' Her escort, who had a pair of small and greedy eyes fixed on Deborah's breasts, muttered something, and Renata leaned over Louis and caught his chin, trying to turn his face up to hers. 'What's the matter, Louis, aren't you going to — ugh!' She snatched her hand away as if Louis had been red-hot and displayed a palm sticky with icecream. She turned to Deborah. 'Really, Miss Barnett, I should have thought your first task would have been to see that the child was clean! You've nothing else to do!'

'It isn't dirt, Mrs Brightmore, it's icecream,' Deborah said calmly. 'It's almost impossible for a five-year-old to eat it without getting some round his mouth.'

'But I didn't touch his mouth,' Renata protested. She gave an exaggerated shudder and produced a tiny lace handkerchief beginning, ostentatiously, to wipe her hands with it. 'Tom, when are you going to come and see me? I'll tell you what, why not come to Desmond's party tonight? He'd love that, wouldn't you, Dessy?'

Desmond, coming abruptly out of his trance, assured them that he would be delighted to see them both at his party that evening but Tom said very civilly that, speaking for himself, he was far too busy at this time of year for socialising in the evenings, especially when Monsieur Frenaye was away from the estate.

Renata appeared not to hear Deborah's murmur that she could not leave Louis, or at any rate she did not acknowledge it. She pouted at Tom.

'You're a spoilsport, Tom Saunders, no one can be *that* busy! Anyway, you're socialising now, aren't you?' Then, when Tom merely smiled but refused to comment, she turned to Deborah. 'Oh, Miss Barnett, do clean the boy up before you take him into the street! Someone might recognise him, and he *is* my nephew!'

'What a . . . what an unusual person she is,' Deborah remarked as she and Tom resumed their seats once more and began to sip their tea. 'Never at a loss for a cutting remark, I'd guess. And who was that gormless twit she had in tow?'

'That's Desmond Gibbon. He's immensely rich, and has a yacht in the harbour bigger than my whole house. But does he live on it? Not he. He has a suite in the most expensive hotel on the island. I rather wonder what Renata's up to, though. When Guy's in residence, she spends all her time at his elbow. I've always assumed that she's ready and waiting, with her answer all ready, for the question to be popped.'

'Perhaps she's decided that a yacht and a private suite outstrip sugar plantations and Paris offices,' Deborah said nastily. 'Though how anyone could contemplate any sort of relationship with that slimy little man I do not know!'

'You didn't like him eyeing your assets,' Tom said, grinning. 'Don't worry, it's a compliment!' He turned to Louis. 'Finished, old man? Then shall we go?'

Louis remained quiet and subdued until they reached the animal market, when his good spirits abruptly returned, so that they did an exhaustive, and exhausting, tour of all the cages and boxes and bowls, though it was to one particular occupant that Louis was mostly drawn. A big wicker cage housed a collection of puppies, amongst which was a white ball of fluff with round, bright eyes and a lolling pink tongue. Seeing Louis on his knees by the pup, his fingers thrust wistfully through the bars to touch the dandelion clock of its head, Deborah vowed to herself that as soon as Monsieur Frenaye seemed approachable, she would try to get permission for Louis to own a pet. If he had something of his own to love, she thought, he would spend less time with Essie and Prince Charles. She no longer thought for one moment that Essie's influence was baleful, but she was not unwilling to use Monsieur Frenaye's prejudices on the side of more fun for Louis.

'Well, old man, all good things must come to an end, and you're already late for your tea,' Tom said cheerfully, after an hour of peering into cages. 'Never mind, eh? Next time mademoiselle comes shopping,

54

you and I will come here again. What do you say to that?'

Louis nodded enthusiastically, but his footsteps dragged a little as they made their way through the town.

'He's tired,' Deborah said, as they left the market far behind and neared the harbour once more. 'It's been a marvellous afternoon for us both, Tom. Thank you so much for making it possible.'

Tom glanced down at Louis, clinging to Deborah's hand. His thumb was in his mouth and his eyelids drooped, but he looked supremely happy and was crooning a song about mice and windmills in Old Amsterdam beneath his breath.

'Taking you two out is a pleasure, and I mean that. Here, old boy, I'll give you a lift.'

He swung Louis into his arms, then struck out an elbow and nodded to it. 'Hang on to me, Deborah, and we'll be back at the harbour in no time.'

Threading through the crowded, busy streets of the shopping centre, Deborah thought how like a family group they must seem, and smiled to herself. Ridiculous, with she and Tom both fair and Louis so dark, but she could tell by the indulgent glances cast at Louis's sleeping form, that most people thought they were his parents.

'Can you take him without waking him?' Tom murmured as they reached the car. 'That's right, gently does it. Now you slip into the passenger seat and I'll drive slowly and with luck, we'll get home without waking my laddo.' As they performed this manoeuvre, he patted her shoulder. 'Well done! I suppose you wouldn't like to complete my day by coming to the flicks with me this evening?'

'I'd love to, but no chance I'm afraid; I wouldn't like to leave Louis with Suzanne on the spur of the moment. But another day, well, I'd love to. Perhaps we could leave it until Monsieur Frenaye gets back?'

'All right, if you'd prefer it. Or we could get Mrs Brightmore to babysit!'

He was teasing, but Deborah felt her heart miss a beat.

'Oh no, I wouldn't subject Louis to that!'

'But Deborah, suppose they marry, Renata and Frenaye?'

Deborah's heart gave an apprehensive lurch, though she answered Tom casually enough. And after Tom had left her and she was waving him off, the thought crossed her mind that perhaps now his English was so notably improved, Louis might learn to put up with his aunt. It gave her no comfort, though it should have done.

4

To Deborah's relief, the front door was slightly ajar, so she did not have to risk waking Louis by knocking or ringing. She would, she decided, slip straight up to the boy's room and pop him into bed, then tidy herself before going down to tell Suzanne that she was back and would be glad of a simple meal. Tea had been missed, perhaps, but Louis had eaten the icecream and two cream cakes, besides drinking a good deal of orange juice, so was unlikely to be woken by hunger pangs.

She stole across the hall, up the stairs, and into Louis's room. Sitting on the bed with the boy on her lap, she slid him out of his T-shirt and shorts, pulled off his sandals, and put on his soft, buttonless pyjamas. That performed without causing the small slumberer to do more than murmur, she popped him into bed, then went quietly to the window and pulled down the blind, fixing it so that air could come in but insects could not. Then she pulled the curtains as quietly as possible and crossed the darkened room to look down on her small charge. So dirty! Smears of icecream, dirt from the shop windows he had pressed against, stray hairs from the many puppies caressed and kittens cuddled, Louis had managed to acquire them all. But his cheeks were flushed and his expression was still blissfully happy.

One last glance round to check that all was in order, and then Deborah backed out of the room, deciding to leave the door slightly ajar just in case Louis awoke and wanted her, though it seemed very unlikely in view of the way he had slept so far. She was about to turn and descend the stairs when a voice spoke close to her ear.

'Where have *you* been?'

She jumped and gasped, then spun round to face the intruder, and felt her heartbeat slow to normal.

'Monsieur Frenaye, what a fright you gave me! I've just put Louis to bed.'

He took her arm, leading her towards the stairs, for they had both kept their voices low, in deference to the sleeping child.

'I did not mean where have you been at this moment, mademoiselle, I meant where have you been all afternoon? I came back here expecting to find you and my son, and the house was empty. Not much of a welcome for a prodigal father.'

'Goodness, yes, I told Suzanne that since we were going out she and Poppy might as well take the afternoon off,' Deborah admitted. She glanced sideways at him. More tanned than ever, he was immaculate in a cream linen jacket and chocolate brown slacks, but she thought she could detect weariness in the line of his mouth. 'Have you been back long, monsieur? If you'd let someone know you were coming, we would have stayed at home.'

'I didn't know myself until this morning. Now come along, tell me where you've been.'

He led her into the cool, green curtained living room with its long French windows opening on to the terrace. They were open now, and a pleasant breeze blew in, reducing the warmth of the atmosphere appreciably. As they entered the room, Monsieur

Frenaye tugged at the bell-pull by the door and when Suzanne appeared, said, 'The drinks trolley, please,' before settling down on the silk upholstered couch and patting the cushion next to his.

'Come and sit down, Deborah, and tell me where you've been.'

'I've been into Castlebridge. I took Louis, of course.'

He glanced narrowly at her. There was something in his expression which she could not interpret.

'Oh, yes? You went by bus, I suppose? Or did you get a car?'

'We had a car.' She did not want to tell him that Tom Saunders had taken her into town for it had just occurred to her that Tom, in fact, might get into trouble for just leaving the office and taking her shopping and sightseeing.

'And then?'

'We went round Thirsk's, and Manilow's, and round those little shops by the harbour. Oh, and we trekked up to the animal market because Louis loves it there. I saw the dreamiest dress in a place opposite a chap selling live lobsters, but I didn't buy it, far too expensive, and then we came home. What else should I have done?'

'You might have had tea, perhaps. I daresay Louis was hungry.'

It was said casually enough, but warning lights of vivid red flashed in Deborah's brain. That bitch had seen him already, an inner voice warned.

'Yes, of course, I'd almost forgotten, we did have tea. At an awfully smart place, overlooking the harbour. Louis had a dish of multi-coloured ice-cream and Tom and I had tea and cakes.'

'Precisely. Why did you not mention that it was Saunders who took you into town, mademoiselle?'

Previous experience had taught Deborah that it was usually a lot less complicated to tell the truth right from the start. Now she had confirmed the fact. Not that she had lied, but she had suppressed the truth, with the best possible motive, of course.

'Well, Monsieur Frenaye, you are Mr Saunders' employer, and it occurred to me that perhaps he should not have taken the afternoon off to go round the shops with me. But I wasn't deliberately keeping the information from you, especially since Louis would be bound to mention it tomorrow.'

'You think so?' Dark brows rose cynically. 'My son would tell me only that which you wished told, I've no doubt.'

'That, monsieur, is unfair both to your son and to myself. Louis would speak the truth instinctively and I would never encourage the boy to lie, particularly to his father. Really, Monsieur Frenaye, what do you think of me?'

He smiled. 'Only that you are a woman, mademoiselle. Women, I know, do not always feel that truth is important if it is also inconvenient! So you went shopping with Saunders and the boy. I've no objection to that, but — '

'I should hope not!' Deborah said indignantly. 'And if you're going to point out, monsieur, that it was not *my* afternoon off, even if it was Mr Saunders', then I'd like to point out that I've been here eight days and haven't taken so much as half an hour off! Anyway, Louis was with me and still very much my responsibility.'

'Why is this? Surely you do not pretend that there was no one who could be left with the boy?'

'You'd made no arrangements about the payment of my salary, so I had no money,' Deborah flashed angrily. 'You'd said nothing about leaving Louis with the servants, so I didn't like to do so, and I didn't know when you might come back or where I might turn for help and advice, so — '

'The drinks, monsieur, and a few savouries. Dinner will be served in an hour.'

Deborah, who was starving, bit back an exclamation of dismay and then, after a glance at the trolley, decided that dinner could be put off for two hours provided she was to be allowed her way with the savouries. Crab puffs, short lengths of celery stuffed with cream cheese and decorated with tiny half-moons of red pepper, little sandwiches and tiny sausage rolls were set out on plates, looking mouth-wateringly delicious.

'A long drink, mademoiselle, or do you prefer spirits?'

'A long drink would be lovely, thank you,' Deborah said hopefully. 'Orange juice and soda water is nice.'

He pulled a face. 'It sounds very ... English, mademoiselle.' He poured her drink, handed it to her, and returned to his seat on the couch. 'Now, let us return to your grievances.'

'Well, you went off and left me without any money or proper instructions, yet you come home unexpectedly and feel entitled to cross-question me closely on trival matters, like where I've been and with whom. That's one grievance.'

She stood up, and took a plate, then chose a selection of savouries from the trolley. 'Do you want something, monsieur?'

'Yes, I'll have a selection like yours.' He sounded amused, but she obeyed him silently, then sat down again and began to eat. 'Now, Miss Barnett, we'll dispose of a few of your misconceptions for a start. I did make arrangements so that you might have some time to yourself. As I told you, Mrs Brightmore agreed to spend every afternoon with Louis, and to arrange with Tom to pay your salary. Unfortunately, my sister-in-law found herself so heavily committed that she was unable to get away. Renata is a partner. in a dress shop down by the harbour. Her partner, Madame Dumart, was called away on business, so Renata, who does not usually work in the shop, was left in charge. Thus her time was not her own.'

'I see. I suppose it never occurred to her to telephone me and explain, or to telephone Mr Saunders, for that matter, and let him know the plight I was in?'

'But naturally! That is what she did, and why Saunders came round to the house and gave you some money.'

Deborah shook her head, at the same time swallowing a crab puff practically intact, so great was her indignation. 'She did not! I went down to the estate office, and I had to explain to Tom that I had no money, which wasn't very pleasant, but fortunately he understood at once and forwarded me thirty pounds.'

She got to her feet and scooped more sausage rolls on to her plate. Suzanne was a marvellous cook. A glance at Monsieur Frenaye as she took her place on the couch again confirmed that he looked a bit taken aback.

'Oh, so that was the way of it. Renata did not, in fact . . . But you must not blame me entirely for what amounts to bad management. Was it wise to run out of money completely? Suppose I had intended to pay your salary monthly!'

'Your mother told me I'd be paid weekly, and advised me to get some summery clothing before I left London. In mid-January, monsieur, shopping for the summer can be an expensive business, and I am not old enough to have accrued much in the way of savings. But I think we've strayed from the point. You could have telephoned me, I assume, since you spoke to Tom last night. It would have relieved my mind a good deal, since the entire responsibility for the house and your son has seemed very heavy these past eight days.'

'Yes, very well, you've made yourself crystal clear.' He sounded annoyed and Deborah thought with satisfaction that, however much he disliked being in the wrong, he was going to have to concede this round to her. She reckoned, however, without Renata's contribution. 'Whilst we're on the subject of Louis and your responsibilities, I'd like to point out that whilst I'm only too happy for you to take the boy into Castlebridge with you, you must make sure he's clean and respectable before taking him into a popular tea-room.'

'He *was* clean and respectable,' Deborah protested. 'At least, he was when we went in. He had a dish of multi-coloured icecream, though, and there were traces of it on his face when your sister-in-law approached us.'

'Hm. Renata said the boy was filthy and looked a regular little ragamuffin. Don't let it occur again, please.'

Deborah was eating a shrimp boat. It was similar to a vol-au-vent in that a pastry case held shrimps in a tasty pink sauce, but instead of puff pastry, it had a rich biscuit crust. It was her third. Now, she sat very still, gripping her hands together in her lap, whilst the shrimp boat, previously so delicious, turned to ashes in her mouth.

'Monsieur Frenaye, Louis did not look like a ragamuffin!' She almost shouted the words in her determination to force belief. 'He looked like any other small boy who's been eating icecream.'

In her eagerness to make her point her hands were balled into fists, her face was pink. She saw his gaze drop from her face to her hands, then back again. He was smiling.

'You are so much in earnest, mademoiselle, that I'm sure you're telling the truth as you see it.' He got to his feet. 'I'll see you at dinner.' The expressive eyes flickered down again, to her clenched fists. He passed a hand across his mouth. 'You'll have had a good wash by then, I trust!'

She followed his glance. In one clenched fist the remains of a shrimp boat was squashed to an unidentifiable pulp.

* * *

As a result of their earlier confrontation, dinner was rather a difficult meal. Deborah put on her blue, off-the-shoulder dress and a pair of navy pin-heeled sandals, but not all the sophistication in the world could quite banish from her memory the fate of the shrimp boat. Monsieur Frenaye, however, seemed to be wrapped in thought and though those thoughts sent his glance across to Deborah several times, there was neither suppressed amusement nor animosity in his eyes. And with the arrival of a lemon chiffon pudding which melted in the mouth, he seemed to rouse himself from his abstraction and began to question Deborah about Louis's progress. How was his son's English progressing, did he yet know any English fairy tales, was he spending as much time with Essie as formerly, and finally, what did the two of them do with themselves in the afternoons.

Deborah enumerated their various pastimes,

including their daily swim, but this brought the scowl back into being once more.

'Swimming? Judging by your ability, it might be wiser, mademoiselle, if you and Louis waited until either myself or Renata were present before taking to the water. You are too timid and Louis is too fearless, to be blunt.'

'Very well, monsieur. I'll explain to Louis.'

He glanced at her as if expecting some further argument or explanation, then raised his brows.

'What, no protestation that you are quite capable, no reasoned harangue in your own defence? I'm surprised at you, mademoiselle; I didn't think you'd give in so easily. Surely you want to point out that you are quite capable of curbing Louis's fearlessness? That you would never let him risk his life, and that his professed dislike of Renata might lead to far worse consequences than your presence in the water?'

It was now Deborah's turn to pin a look of courteous surprise to her face and to infuse her voice with as much innocence as possible.

'Why should I protest, monsieur, when you are right, and I know it? Louis would be far safer, in the sea, with either yourself or Mrs Brightmore. You'll find I'm never unreasonable, monsieur, nor will I ever raise my voice against commonsense and intelligent persuasion.'

He grinned appreciatively across the table.

'Only against foolishness and stupidity, I infer?' He stood up and came round the table as she, too, rose to her feet. He took her shoulders and turned her gently round to face him, looking down at her with a wry smile. 'So pretty and demure, a picture in white, gold and blue, but sharp to cut the hand! A fascinating combination.'

Her face was tilted up, her mouth tilting into a smile. Words were on her lips to answer him pertly, when she saw the look on his face change subtly, and saw his head begin to lower itself to hers. Her words faltered and were silenced as his mouth took hers.

Immediately, the magic claimed her. His mouth was demanding, his hands moved across the smooth bareness of her back, gripping her so close that she could feel the warmth and hardness of his body through the thin cotton of her dress. He parted her lips and she tried, half-heartedly, to pull away even as he deepened the kiss and one hand came up to caress the back of her neck, fingers pushing up into her hair.

One minute they were kissing, standing pressed against the dining table. The next, she felt herself scooped up into his arms and then she was laid, none too gently, upon the big, soft sofa, with his weight on her. Her body seemed to melt into the cushions, his mouth moved on hers and his hand caressed the swell of her breasts above her brief little satin bra. She tugged at his shoulders, then wrenched her mouth free as his lips began to travel, hot and exciting, across her throat.

'Monsieur Frenaye, please! This is most . . . '

He propped himself up on one elbow. His face had a sleepy, satisfied look, his eyes gleamed beneath lowered lips. One brow lifted with faint arrogance.

'Yes, Miss Barnett? Were you trying to attract my attention? Or perhaps, in the circumstances, I might call you Deborah!'

'I think in the circumstances you'd better get up and let me follow suit,' Deborah said crisply, but with hammering heart. 'Really, monsieur, you shouldn't . . . '

'Why not? You enjoy it, I enjoy it, and we are

harming no one.' His eyes dropped from hers, to travel over her mouth, her throat, down to the warm darkness of the cleavage between her breasts. His eyes brought a blush burning across the white flesh and she wriggled, horrified at the desire in her which tempted her not only to admit enjoyment, but to continue to enjoy.

'You shouldn't make love to me. I'm your employee. May I get up, please?'

The blue eyes above her own were every bit as wicked as Louis's could be on occasion, she thought. He did not move, but the arm which was beneath her propped her up a bit more, thrusting against her shoulder blades so that her breasts pushed forward, straining against the thin cotton of her dress. He dropped his head and she felt his mouth hot against the skin of her upper breasts. She gasped, a surge of feeling crashing through her, like a wave against the shore. His free hand slid inside the dress, into the cup of her bra, lifting her breast into his palm, whilst his mouth moved on her, burning kisses, making her moan involuntarily, even token resistance fled beneath the pleasure his mouth was bringing.

When he moved away from her and suddenly dragged her upright into a sitting position, she was shocked to hear voices in the hall and to realise that she had been oblivious of everyone and everything, caring for nothing except what he was doing to her. She blinked and knew she blushed, but all she could do was pull her frock straight and try, with trembling fingers, to tidy her hair. She knew that her lips would be swollen, that her hands trembled, her heartbeat could almost be seen as it began, at last, to slow. But Monsieur Frenaye was composed, getting to his feet, moving across the room.

'Rosa, how nice to see you! Is Renata with you?'

Deborah got to her feet and saw that the visitor was alone, a small, slim brunette of forty or so with a thin, intelligent face and bright eyes. Suzanne, who must have opened the front door to her, was standing in the hallway. He turned to her. 'Coffee for three please, Suzanne.' He took the small woman's arm and led her right into the dining room. 'You've not met Miss Deborah Barnett yet, I believe. She looks after Louis for me. Deborah, this is Rosa Dumart, my sister-in-law's friend and business partner.'

Deborah held out her hand and smiled. She hoped she looked calm and collected but feared she looked hot, flustered, and all but seduced. However, Madame Dumart smiled and shook her hand, giving her the quick, appraising glance that one attractive woman gives another. There was no hint, in that glance, that she thought she had interrupted anything save a quiet dinner for two.

'How do you do, Miss Barnett, or may I call you Deborah? Do call me Rosa. We are very informal, you'll find, on the island, and first names are almost universally used. I came over because my husband and I are giving a barbecue party in a couple of days and Renata mentioned that there was a new young lady at Frèremaison. I wanted to make sure that Guy would bring you to my party.' She patted Deborah's hand and led her back to the sofa. Deborah sat down on it with very different emotions to those which had warred in her breast as she leaped off it two minutes earlier! 'Now that I've seen you, my dear, I know you'll make my party a great success if you attend it, so you must promise to bring her, Guy. I have a great many young men coming, all of whom adore natural blondes.'

'I'd love to come, but what about Louis?' said Deborah, glancing at her employer out of the corner of her eye. 'I've not left him at all, yet.'

'Then it's high time you did,' Monsieur Frenaye said rather curtly. He strolled across to the doorway. 'Amuse each other for a few moments, ladies, whilst I go and remind Suzanne that our visitor is a Frenchwoman, so might well appreciate black coffee.'

'Don't you dare disappear before you've agreed that Deborah can come to my party, Guy,' commanded the older woman. 'She has a conscience, this one, and will turn me down if she feels it her duty to remain with the boy.'

'Of course she'll come, it's about time she had some social life,' Monsieur Frenaye said. 'What with your business taking you to Paris, and Renata forgetting to telephone through to my estate manager and explain, she's had a dull enough time so far, not meeting a soul bar the boy. Excuse me whilst I organise this coffee!'

He left the room and Rosa turned enquiringly to Deborah. Her clothes, Deborah noticed enviously, were exquisitely cut and she had a frilly blouse which was out of this world, but now she looked puzzled.

'My absence in Paris? What does he mean? I've not been to Paris for over a month. As for Renata not telephoning, why should she have done so? She's been out almost every day with that little fellow from the yacht. And why should this effect your social life?'

'There was a misunderstanding, I believe,' Deborah said vaguely. 'Monsieur Frenaye was away on business himself all last week, he's only just returned. I daresay he's got confused.'

'Hm. It isn't like Guy to muddle dates. What have you been doing with yourself this past week, my dear? I hope you and the boy are getting on well? I saw Essie's cottage as I drove up from the McMahon's place, and remembered that she's living there all the time now she's been pensioned off. But I daresay she'd babysit for you if you couldn't get one of the servants to oblige.'

'I haven't done a lot, but Louis and I get on awfully well,' Deborah said, warming to the other's obvious interest. 'Did Essie live in, then, when she was Louis's nurse? I hadn't realised, especially since her cottage seems as though it's been there for ever!'

'She lived in four nights a week, and went to her cottage the other three, I believe,' Rosa said. 'She took Louis with her, back to the cottage, until Guy moved back here, though. There was a nursery maid, too, a pretty thing out from England called Ada. There was some scandal, I can't call to mind exactly what, and she left. Guy never did replace her, which is why, I suppose, Essie became such a force to be reckoned with in the boy's life.'

'Louis has never mentioned Ada, but of course his talk was full of Essie, especially at first: She still means a lot to him, but he's getting his love for her in proportion. She's a good woman, and knows that he'll grow away from her. So long as it's a natural growth and not the result of being forced to keep away from her she's quite happy with the situation.'

'You sound as though you approve of Essie. Renata was sure she was a bad influence on the boy.'

'Not at all,' Deborah said firmly. 'I not only approve of Essie, I like her. She's a strong woman with a good deal of character, and she has something which appeals even more than strength of character to a five-year-old.'

'Oh, what's that?'

Deborah smiled. 'Prince Charles. Louis finds him irresistible, to say nothing of a litter of patch-work kittens!'

'Prince Charles, did you say?'

'Prince Charles is the name given to a wild-eyed mongrel cur which leaped upon my person and covered my white drill trousers with mud on the only occasion I visited Essie's home.' Guy Frenaye came through the doorway, propelling the trolley set with coffee, after-dinner mints and petit fours. He brought the trolley to a halt beside the sofa, then pulled up an easy chair and sank into it. 'Would you pour the coffee please, Miss Barnett?'

Deborah happened to be watching the French-woman, and saw the mobile, black eyebrows draw into a tiny frown. She was wondering why, when Rosa said abruptly, 'You're a strange man, Guy! Did you say that you'd bring Deborah to my party?'

Deborah, pouring coffee, saw quick comprehension dawn. He smiled a trifle wolfishly, she felt.

'Naturally. And we will dispense with formality now, Deborah, so that we can both enjoy this party. You had better call me Guy.'

'Very well, monsieur,' Deborah said composedly, handing round the coffee and the thick cream in the small silver jug. Her hackles had risen at the slight air of condescension she fancied she had heard in his tone. She was good enough to tumble on the couch, good enough to seduce, but it had taken a colossal hint from an old friend before he suggested that she should use his given name! I shan't call him anything at all, she told herself crossly. Certainly I shan't call him Guy; it's a stupid name!

Having issued her invitation and drunk her coffee, Madame Dumart got to her feet.

71

'You aren't quite my last call,' she said gaily, as they moved into the hall to see her off. 'I have to go right along the coast road to the Howards' place. They've let it to three charming young Americans; I want them to come along to my party.'

'Wouldn't you rather I passed your invitation on?' Guy said solicitously. 'The road's bad for night driving, even though there's a moon. I'll go up there tonight willingly, if you wish me to.'

Rosa smiled at him, but shook her head.

'No thank you, Guy. I prefer to go myself and get an immediate response. Look what happened with Renata. She promised faithfully that she would remind you to bring Deborah, and obviously completely forgot about it. Goodnight to you both.'

As the door was closed behind the visitor, Deborah glanced at her wristwatch, then turned towards the stairs. It was well past her bedtime, and Louis was always awake at six and eager for her to wake as well. But with her foot on the bottom stair, she was called back in a very imperious voice.

'Deborah! Come into the living room for a moment, if you please.'

Obediently, she followed him into the large and pleasant room. He was turning off the lights, all except one dim lamp, and closing the French windows, though he left the small side windows open for the air to circulate. Then he walked over to the wide green couch and sat down, patting the cushion next to him.

'Over here, please, mademoiselle.'

Deborah, completely unsuspecting, obeyed. He promptly put his arms round her.

'I apologise for the interruption. Now where were we?'

Deborah kicked him smartly in the shins and shot

72

across to the opposite end of the couch. She was breathing hard and her cheeks were hot.

'Really, monsieur, I'm not a plaything, to be picked up and put down when you choose! If you have nothing else to say to me, I'm going to bed.'

His hands shot out and grasped her wrists. He was smiling, but she could sense that his breathing, too, had quickened.

'I could scarcely have retained my hold on you in the circumstances, ma mie! What would Rosa have thought if I had not, in fact, put you down? You may not mind an audience, but . . . '

Deborah struggled vainly to free herself for a moment, then she sighed and rolled her eyes ceilingwards.

'I thought I'd made it plain, monsieur, that I didn't wish you to make love to me. The episode in the dining room took place by your insistence, not mine. I kept asking you to let me up, but – '

'How adorable you look when you're lying! And how bright your eyes are when you're angry!' He pulled her closer and the teasing look fled from his face, to be replaced by an expression she recognised. An anticipatory look. 'You're a beautiful girl with a beautiful body and you enjoy lovemaking. I'll show you.'

His mouth was persuasive, insistent, and she wanted to succumb, to lie back on the soft cushions and let him love her. But the recollection of some of the things he had said to her when she returned from Castlebridge came to her rescue. She dragged herself out of his arms with a thumping heart, trembling but resolute.

'Stop it! I'm here to look after your son, not to have a casual affair with you.' She stood up, then put out a hand to fend him off as he, too, rose to his feet. 'I will see you, monsieur, in the morning.'

He caught her arm as she whipped past him, nearly wrenching it out of its socket.

'Ouch! Take your hands off me!' Her voice was shrill. For the first time, she felt afraid of him.

'Certainly, when you use my name, as I told you to.' His eyes were glittering, his mouth held a harsh line. She could see that he was angered, both by her refusal to allow him to continue his lovemaking and by her determined use of his title. And since she dared not let him continue to make love to her, she had better give in gracefully over the other matter.

'I'm very sorry. Goodnight, Guy.' She spoke stiffly, then sighed and smiled up at him. 'Look, I think English girls must be very different in their approach to men and love from French ones. We do like to think we have some say in who makes love to us; we don't much like just being pounced on.'

He nodded, releasing her arm.

'So you say. Very well, I'll bear it in mind. Goodnight, Deborah.'

Once in her room, Deborah got herself to bed and then snuggled down, to enjoy the luxury of some serious speculation. It was true that she found it difficult to repulse her employer when he made love to her, but that, surely, was merely a physical reaction to an experienced man who knew how to please women? Had she, by that physical reaction, led him on? She had not meant to do so since she had no desire whatsoever to end up in his bed, knowing that he already had a relationship with Renata. It would only make her life at Frère-maison incredibly difficult, for he was very much her employer, an arrogant and dictatorial man who certainly would not consider the world well lost for his son's nanny!

She decided, after some more cogitation, that in fact she was probably making a mountain out of a molehill. After all, a good many men seemed to think it their duty to try to make love to any attractive girl who came within their orbit, although they had no intention of compromising themselves by attempting a seduction. Probably, he just enjoyed kissing and cuddling, and would not attempt to take it further.

She sighed. The trouble was, he was not the only one who liked kissing and cuddling, and she had no intention of falling in love with someone who was so incredibly handsome, and so incredibly entangled with another woman!

The best thing to do, of course, would be to find someone of around her own age who would take her out a few times. Then she could make it plain to Monsieur Frenaye that he was trespassing. She did not doubt for one moment that, in those circumstances, he would draw back. Men might have strange morals, but they usually behaved quite reasonably towards each other.

The rest of the time before she fell asleep was spent in the delightful pastime of imagining herself, in that white dress which she had not been able to afford, in the arms of a young and handsome man who would make Monsieur Frenaye see what he had missed.

5

'But why, mademoiselle, can you not tell me a story? Just a little one! Just a teeny weeny one! Oh, Deb-or-ah, the three billy goats gruff are so sweet, with their tippy tappy toes! Oh, please, mademoiselle!'

Louis stared imploringly up into Deborah's face, dancing up and down on his own tippy tappy toes, his large blue eyes pleading. Deborah sighed. She had bathed him, powdered him, popped him into his pyjamas and gone down to the kitchen so that he could have his milk and biscuits earlier than usual, for tonight was the night of the Dumarts' barbecue party. Guy had told her to be ready and waiting for him when he returned to the house at seven o'clock, and it was already half past six. She had not showered or done her hair, and though her apricot silk dress was laid out ready on her bed and her shoes nearby, the new clutch bag, the new lipstick, were still in the shop's bags. But Louis must come first!

'All right, mon brave, but you must pop into bed, and I'll bring my party clothes through into your room and change in there. I've got to have a shower, now, but that won't take five minutes. How does that suit you?'

Louis dived into her bedroom ahead of her.

'I'll take your clo'ses to my room! Is it th-this dress? These shoes?'

His English was improving by leaps and bounds, and he used it more naturally, too. Deborah, following him in, nodded.

'That's right. Now pop into bed and eat your bickies; there are two sorts, because you didn't eat much at teatime. And don't save any for Prince Charles, because if you keep giving him sweet things he'll be toothless before he's twenty.'

'Really? Will his teez really fall out?'

'Teeth, petit chou, teeth with a th!' Deborah picked up her towel and made for the shower. She left the door of the small cabinet ajar, however, and raised her voice so that he could hear her above the patter of the water. 'No, they probably won't fall out, but sweet things aren't good for dogs and they are good for you. Well, fairly good. Anyway, just eat them up!'

Presently, showered, talcumed and perfumed, she returned to his room, having first put on her white lace bra and matching briefs. Her hair was damp still, but curling under, so though it might not look its best, it would be presentable, at any rate.

'Now, mademoiselle!' Louis sat up straighter, his small sturdy body alert and expectant. 'Once upon a time there were free — three — billy goats gruff, and they — '

'Who's telling this story?' Deborah's voice was muffled by the dress which she was pulling down over her head. 'Once upon a time, there were three billy goats gruff . . . '

By the time the dress was on, her hair thoroughly dry and her sandals donned, the story was over. But Louis was all agog to watch the rest of her preparations, so she improved the shining hour by telling him a new story, the story of Cinderella, since it seemed appropriate. Sitting in front of Louis's small dressing table and mirror she applied lipstick and brushed mascara on to her thick, light lashes, giving Cinderella, in addition to the usual attributes, an intelligent and friendly dog called Prince Charles. She knew her charge too well to think that he would be thrilled at the prospect of the heroine marrying a mere prince, but if one were to bend the story a little — have the dog rescue Cinderella from the wicked sisters and eventually, upon being the recipient of a kiss, change into a handsome prince — that would make the story every bit as satisfactory as the three billy goats gruff.

She was concluding the tale with a flourish when she turned from the mirror and saw that her audience had doubled. Guy stood there, leaning against the door jamb, his hands thrust into his pockets, a quizzical grin on his face.

'Really, Deborah, whatever happened to the good old glass slipper? Prince Charles gets in everywhere these days, now you'll have Louis kissing the brute as well as admiring him.'

'I won't, Papa!' Louis bounced out of his bed and ran across to his father, grabbing at the sleeve of his white dinner jacket. 'I wouldn't want my dear Prince Charles to turn into a *man*! But it's a good story, that. Tomorrow morning, after we've had a swim, I'll tell it to Essie.'

'I daresay she'll be quite surprised,' Guy said dryly. 'Come along, mon vieux, back to bed. I am about to take this Cinderella to the ball, and we don't want to miss the pumpkin!'

Louis, struggling back into bed, giggled.

'And will you kiss her, Papa? If you do, perhaps

she'll turn into a dog with big, big ears and lovely brown eyes!'

'In that case I'll be very careful not to kiss her. Goodnight Louis.'

He bent over the boy, rumpled his hair, and kissed her forehead. Deborah thought that it was the first time she had ever seen Guy kiss his son. She followed him over to the bed.

'Goodnight, sweetheart. Don't wake me *too* early in the morning, will you? I daresay it will be quite late before your Papa and I get home.'

'We-ell . . . ' he smiled up at her, his eyes sparkling mischievously. 'I will try to stay in bed. And I'd rather have you even than Prince Charles, mademoiselle, so don't let my Papa kiss you!'

'Nothing,' Deborah assured him solemnly, 'is further from my thoughts. Sweet dreams, mon petit.'

They were leaving the room when Louis remembered something.

'Mademoiselle, say our poem — our goodnight poem.'

Guy stood in the doorway watching his son, and there was tenderness in the glance which rested on the dark head. Deborah sighed. She had a strong feeling that Guy would not altogether approve of their night time poem.

'Night night, sleep tight, please make sure the bugs don't bite,' she chanted.

As they descended the stairs, Guy glanced at her.

'Now why that particular rhyme, mademoiselle?' he asked plaintively. 'He's certain to come out with it at some inappropriate moment. There must be other rhymes.'

'There are, heaps,' Deborah assured him. 'But children being children, that was the one Louis liked best.' She was truly thankful that Louis had refrained from leaping up and down in the bed and scratching imaginary bug-bites, as he sometimes did.

'Then I must absolve you from blame, I suppose.' They reached the hallway, crossed it, and walked over to where the car was parked, waiting for them. 'And I must remember not to kiss you.'

'That goes without saying.' Deborah got into the car. 'We'll both obey the rules, monsieur, and I'm sure we'll have a delightful evening.' She leaned back in her seat and smiled demurely across at him. 'Didn't Madame Dumart say that there would be three young Americans present? What more could I ask for?'

He revved the engine and the car moved smoothly away from the house.

'What indeed, Deborah?'

*   *   *

They arrived at the Dumarts' house to find the party already in full swing, with guests milling about the large reception rooms, drinks in hand, whilst below the house, on the beach, others were lighting the huge bonfire which took the place of the more conventional barbecue at the Dumart parties.

'We find nothing equals an open fire with a grill above it,' Rosa told Deborah. 'Come down to the beach with me and I'll introduce you to my husband and some of our guests who are about your age.' She turned to Guy. 'Renata's on the terrace, with Desmond Gibbon. Do let her know you've arrived; you know how edgy she can be.'

'Right,' Guy strolled away from them without a backward glance and Deborah, who had nourished

81

faint hopes that his interest in her might prove more powerful than Renata's sultry charms, chided herself for sheer, crass stupidity, and turned with great vivacity to her hostess.

'This is my first barbecue, Rosa, and I'm looking forward to everything. I'm sure it will be marvellous.'

Monsieur Dumart proved to be a tall, distinguished-looking Frenchman with silver-grey hair and a pleasant personality. He took Deborah under his wing as soon as she appeared on the moonlit beach and introduced her to a dozen husky young men who were helping to carry driftwood from a pile at the top of the beach down to the fire. The three Americans, Ed, Corny and Travers, took her to their hearts at once. Ed was rangy with a drawl and tow-coloured hair, Corny was small and yellow-topped, and Travers had a crew-cut, rimless glasses, and the sort of engaging friendliness which transcends good looks. He used this quality to such good effect that before thirty minutes had elapsed, Deborah found herself sitting on an outcrop of rock with one hand in Travers' and the other holding a glass of champagne.

'You're teaching the little boy English, huh? That'll be Renata's nephew. We've sure heard plenty about his poppa! Nice guy, is he?'

'He's quite nice,' Deborah said cautiously. 'He's my employer, remember, so I wouldn't criticise him anyway.' She turned to Travers. 'Why? What have you heard?'

'Gee, that he's French and dishy, I guess. Renata thinks the world of him; says she fancied him even whilst her sister was around. She quit— the boy's mother, I mean — and Renata started gunning for him. Though that's reading between the lines a bit.'

82

'I had a feeling she couldn't be dead,' Deborah said thoughtfully. 'I thought she was at first but when I got to the house there were no photographs or anything, and no one ever talked about her. I think I probably guessed, then, that she'd left him. How *could* she?' That last, involuntary exclamation made her long to bite it back. What a dam'fool thing to say! It made her sound as if she was leching after the bloke! But Travers saw nothing unusual in her remark.

'He's as handsome as they say, eh? You must point him out to me.'

'Right, I'll do that. How come you know Renata so well though, and haven't even met Guy Frenaye? I thought they went about together a lot?'

Travers laughed. 'Everyone knows Renata, because you meet her everywhere. On the beach, in the hotel bars, at the yacht club — you name a place and if it's fashionable, Renata will be there sooner or later. But Frenaye's got a sugar plantation to run. Renata's a stunner though, isn't she?'

'Oh yes, very,' Deborah said without much enthusiasm. She sipped her champagne. 'I wonder where she is now?'

Travers put his arm round her shoulders and pulled her close. The champagne in Deborah's glass rocked and she drank it quickly before it went all over her new dress.

'Who cares, honey, when we've got each other? With her fella, I guess. Your boss.'

'Yes, I suppose so.' Travers nuzzled the side of her neck and began to kiss her jawline tentatively. 'Gracious, Travers, do stop it, we've only just met! You're a fast worker, aren't you?'

'Huh, be thankful you aren't with Corny! That yaller hair and those wide eyes hide the urges of an alley-cat! C'mon, let's go throw a steak on the grill.'

Later, when she was well fed on the most delicious grilled meat and fish she had ever tasted, there was dancing, and Deborah found herself a popular partner, being pounced on the moment she left the lawn between dances. Rather to her disappointment Tom Saunders was not present, but she found that it was not only the three young Americans who thought her golden head and apricot silk dress attractive. She enjoyed herself enormously, dancing beneath the lanterns which ringed the wide lawn and on the darkened beach, where the younger members of the party played with the bonfire, danced in and out of the creaming surf, and made love in the shadows.

It was here that Guy found her, sitting romantically on the sand with Travers' arm round her, watching the great yellow moon sink towards the sea and trail a path of silver across its wrinkled surface.

'Deborah, it's time we were leaving.'

His tone was peremptory and Deborah scrambled to her feet, disengaging herself from Travers' embrace as discreetly as she could.

'Bye, Travers, and thanks for a lovely evening, but duty calls!' She turned to Guy. 'I'm ready, monsieur.'

He came towards her, putting a casual arm round her waist to lead her away from the bonfire and further up the beach.

'Did you enjoy yourself, Deborah? Who was that young man? You certainly seemed to find his attentions to your taste.'

'He was very nice. Travers, one of those Americans Rosa mentioned. Did you enjoy yourself? And where are we going? The car isn't up here!'

'No, but we can get straight from the beach to the front of the house this way, without having to cross the lawns. I thought it would be easier than saying goodnight all over again.'

Deborah stopped short.

'Oh heavens, but I've not said goodnight to anyone, or thank you! I *must* go back the other way, truly, Guy!'

He looked down at her, a gleam in his eyes. He was so close that she could feel his breath on her forehead.

'Oh very well, in a minute. But I want to talk to you first.'

'Go ahead, then, talk.'

He sighed and slid his hands round her waist and up her back, pulling her closer still.

'This is party talk. It's much more fun than ordinary talk.'

But his lips had barely claimed hers before there was a scuffle behind them and a voice, pitched high, called out, 'Guy darling, what *are* you up to? Where have you gone? Oh, there you are!'

Renata managed to make the last sentence sound as though she had found them in flagrante delicto, but in fact nothing could have been more proper than the way in which they walked towards her, side by side, their hands at least an inch apart.

'Yes, Renata?'

There was definitely a trace of impatience in his voice, Deborah thought joyfully.

'I'm ready to go home now, darling. I thought you said we were leaving.'

'Not you and I, Renata, because you didn't arrive with me. You came with Gibbon. I'm taking Deborah back, now.'

Renata looked marvellous in the fireglow, with

the light adding its own rich overtones to her flaming hair. She was wearing a tight black satin dress which was thoroughly unsuitable for a beach barbecue, but it showed off every curve of her magnificent body. She let her long green eyes flicker disparagingly over Deborah in her apricot silk.

'But I told Desmond you were taking me home. He didn't mind, he knows how things are between us. Besides, I want to talk to you.'

Deborah sensed his indecision and cleared her throat.

'Look, monsieur, don't worry about me, Travers is passing Frèremaison; he can easily take me home.'

She was very sure that, had she not mentioned Travers, he would have agreed to her suggestion. But she saw him stiffen, and shake his head decisively.

'No, I can't do that. I'll arrange for Simon to give you a lift, Renata, if Desmond's already left. He and Gabrielle are passing your hotel and they never mind helping out.'

'It doesn't matter. I'll manage.' She cast a glance acid with dislike at Deborah. 'It was mainly because I wanted to talk to you, Guy!'

'Well, look, I'll come down to your hotel first thing tomorrow morning, we'll have a swim and then talk over breakfast. How will that suit you?'

The cold and furious look faded from Renata's face. She stepped close to Guy, her head bent, looking up at him through her lashes, a slow smile curving her full lips. She was wearing a musky perfume and she exuded sensuality. Deborah instinctively stepped back. So did Guy. The long, pale hands with their scarlet talons which had gone out to grasp the lapels of his dinner jacket were left upraised for a second before they dropped to her sides once more. It had been a rebuff which would have caused Deborah hours of sleeplessness, but Řenata appeared to make it in her stride.

'Oh Guy, what a tease you are! I'll see you tomorrow, then, and mind you're early! I'll go and find Desmond, I think.'

Deborah, feeling very much an intruder, allowed Guy to take her arm and lead her off the beach without making any comment on the scene. He had been polite, but had made it perfectly clear to Renata that he was nobody's property. Renata had been very foolish to try to show her power over someone like Guy in so obvious a fashion, but then a woman in love would often act rashly and unwisely. If, Deborah thought, Renata was capable of loving anyone but herself!

They said their thank yous and goodbyes and Guy helped Deborah into her seat as tenderly as though she was his date for the evening and not just his son's nanny then slid behind the wheel and turned the car towards Frèremaison. When they arrived at the house they went into the hall and he took her hand. Not with any amorous intent, but merely to lead her quietly into the kitchen. Once there, he closed the door softly and clicked on the light.

'Hungry. Or would a drink suffice?' He was smiling down at her, looking so darkly handsome that her heart missed a beat. 'Suzanne's left a flask of hot chocolate and some sandwiches. She always does when I'm out in the evening.'

'I'd love some chocolate,' Deborah admitted. 'Champagne isn't as satisfying as hot chocolate!'

He nodded and moved over to the working surface, pouring hot chocolate into two mugs. He turned, with a mug in either hand and jerked his head at the plate of sandwiches covered with cling film.

'How about one of them? I'm not hungry, but I know you enjoy a snack.'

'No thanks, not at this time of night.'

He raised his brows.

'I can't believe it, I thought your appetite was endless!' He grinned at her blush. 'Never mind, I hate to see women picking at their food. You don't suffer from night starvation, then?'

Deborah took her mug of chocolate and shook her head.

'No, I don't. Why does that sound so sinister, I wonder?'

He grinned but refrained from comment, crossing the hall and leading the way up the stairs. At her door, he stopped.

'Goodnight, Deborah. I'm glad you enjoyed the party.'

She could not have said what she expected, but it was not that he would then walk along the corridor to his own room, without even once glancing back. Putting her drink down on the bedside table, she thought ruefully that this was the nearest she was ever likely to get to a conventional date with her employer, and he had not so much as tried to kiss her goodnight. Plainly he had taken her words to heart, and she would have no more trouble with him.

She hung her dress up in the built-in wardrobe, then stripped and put on a filmy white nightie. Brushing her hair and washing in the quiet moonlight, she decided that she would just check up on Louis before getting into bed. It was not that she didn't trust Suzanne, but she would like to make sure he was all right. She wondered whether they ought to have woken Suzanne, who normally slept in the attic but had moved down into the small room on the far side of Louis's so that she could be near him if he woke, then decided it was not necessary. Suzanne had probably heard them come in, anyway.

The communicating door between her room and Louis's was open, so she went through it and stole softly across the room towards the boy's bed. He was sleeping soundly, his mouth a little open and his thumb lying close to it on the pillow. He sucked his thumb, and she was trying to break him of the habit so, very gently, she took his small paw and tucked it out of sight beneath the covers.

Straightening, she saw his fist appear on the pillow again, the thumb pointing towards his mouth. She smiled to herself, and was about to take action when strong, tanned fingers caught Louis's small hand and tucked it out of harm's way once more.

Her gasp of fright made Guy stare across the short distance which separated them. He put a finger to his lips. then took her wrist, leading her back into her own room. Once there, he pulled the communicating door to, and raised his brows.

'What's the matter? Did I startle you?'

'Yes, you did.' Her heart was still pounding and shock made her tone sharp. 'Wherever did you spring from? One moment I was alone and the next your hand appeared from nowhere. It was very scary.'

'I came in seconds after you did, only I came through the door from the hall. Suzanne had left it open so she could hear if Louis called out. I popped my head round her door to tell her we were back, then came along to check on Louis and close the outer door. The rest you know.' His eyes, which had been on her face, dropped. 'That's a very fetching nightie. I like it even better than your party dress!'

'It's a very ordinary nightie. Goodnight Guy.' They were standing by her bed and she realised she should never have let him lead her in here, not when she was so inadequately clad. But being wise after the event helped no one, she would have to get him out again diplomatically. She glanced hopefully at the door. Why didn't he just *go*?

'Time we went to bed, you think? Goodnight then, chérie.'

She knew that he would kiss her, but not that her state of undress would unleash something in them both. He pulled her close and she heard him groan as he moulded her supple softness against him, his mouth urgent on hers. His kiss, his hands moving hypnotically across her bare back, brought her to a state of breathless pleasure so that when he gently lowered her on to the bed she scarcely realised the implications, certainly suffered no qualms.

'Deborah, ma mie.' He sighed the words as he slid her nightie down off her shoulders, then his hand took her breast, his mouth muffling any protest she might have made.

When his mouth moved from hers, to kiss her throat, the hollows of her collarbones, her breasts, she moaned his name, her fingers tangling in his hair, lost to everything but his lovemaking. His hands slid over her hips, inviting her to push forward against him, to accede to the demand which commonsense told her would presently follow.

They did not hear the door between her room

90

and Louis's open, did not hear the soft patter of his feet as he entered the room. But they both heard his scream. Loud and terrifying, it had them back in their senses, Guy with sufficient command over himself to pull her nightie into respectability before he leapt off the bed and ran across to where Louis was standing in the doorway like a small stone statue, uttering shriek after shriek. Deborah, tumbling on to the floor, her face flushed, her hair untidy, joined them.

'Louis, darling, whatever's the matter?'

Guy hoisted the child into his arms, trying to mould him to his shoulder, a hand caressing the dark head, but Louis stiffened and continued to scream, his mouth square and his eyes tightly shut. Deborah took him from his father, held him against her breast and cuddled him, stroking the hot cheek until his shrieks petered out into sobs of distress.

Guy stood there, watching her. Watching his son. His mouth was grim, and Deborah knew he was blaming himself as bitterly as she blamed herself for her own behaviour.

'Was it a nightmare, mon vieux? You're safe now, safe with Deborah. Come on, let's pop you back into your little bed and you can tell me what upset you.'

Louis's alarming rigidity had gone now. He clung to her, his hot, tear-wet face pressed to hers, snuffling and hiccupping. She popped him between the sheets and sat down on the bed, holding his hand.

'Come on, petit chou. What was it?'

He sighed and carried her hand to his cheek.

'I thought he was eating you! First it was only kisses; he was trying to turn you into a dog like in the story. Then he began to eat you! Oh, mademoiselle, I do love you so much! I don't want you to

91

turn into a dog!' He shuddered, and gulped on another sob. 'And I couldn't bear it if you were eaten!'

'Who was eating me? It was just a bad dream, chéri.'

'I know, now. It was my papa eating you, in my dream.'

Deborah's throat closed with self-disgust, but she forced herself to speak reassuringly, even to tease him a little.

'I should never had told you that silly story, love, not if it's going to give you horrible dreams. Never mind, we all have nightmares, I'll sit with you until you drop off again.'

Stroking his hair as he lay back, Deborah felt ill with horror. To lie there, with the child asleep in the next room, and behave like a wanton with his father! What sort of a woman was she, to throw aside conscience and commonsense alike and give way to animal desires? She shuddered away from what might have happened if he had been a few minutes later in waking up, or less soundly asleep, so that he had known it was no nightmare. Dear God, what had she done?

'She returned to her room when Louis was soundly sleeping, to find Guy sitting on her bed. She longed to hit out at him, blame him for what had happened, but her conscience would not allow such self-deception. She had not made the smallest attempt to stop him, not tonight. She had enjoyed his lovemaking, had been willing for it to continue. Perhaps she would have come to her senses in any case before he carried it to its logical conclusion. But she would never know that.

Guy stood up and took her hands.

'My poor girl, what a dreadful shock! It's useless

to apologise, but the fault was mine, not yours. It was madness to make love to you here, with the child asleep in the next room, but in that flimsy nylon thing . . . It never occurred to me that he might wake. I thought only of how I wanted you.'

'Yes. We were both very much to blame.' She crossed the room to her outer door and held it open for him. 'This must be a lesson to me, and I beg you never to let it happen again.'

'Of course not. Next time . . . '

'There will be no next time, if you please, monsieur. Not a kiss, not a touch. Do you understand?'

He stood in the doorway and touched her hair, his fingers gentle on the silky gold.

'My poor child, you cannot deny your feelings. This was the wrong time and the wrong place but *not* the wrong procedure for two people who want each other. You'll see things more clearly in the morning.'

She did not watch him steal along the corridor to his own room but locked her door and got back into bed. She felt as sinful as if she had in fact allowed him to become her lover, and angry with him now into the bargain. Two people who want each other! She snorted. He wanted her all right — when Renata wasn't around to pout and wriggle at him! But for her part, the icy douche of Louis's terror had put an effective stop to all her desire for Guy's embrace. I'll never be able to sleep because I feel so guilty over Louis, she told herself, lying wide-eyed in the dark.

In fact, exhaustion and unhappiness tipped her into slumber within minutes of getting into bed.

*   *   *

'Good morning, Louis! And how are you this morning? I suppose you've forgotten that you weren't going to wake me until lunchtime?'

Louis was enthroned in the middle of Deborah's stomach, peering down into her face as she opened her eyes for the first time that day. His expression was as sunny and optimistic as though he had never heard the word 'nightmare'.

'Oh, I forgot. But it's sunny, mademoiselle, and we could bathe, perhaps, if you got up right now. I heard Suzanne go down ages ago so we could have our breakfast right away, if we wished! But of course . . . ' his head drooped, ' . . . if you would rather sleep . . . '

'Much chance there is of sleeping, with you about.' Deborah heaved him off on to the floor; then got out of bed. 'Go and wash whilst I have a shower, then we'll put our bathing things on and go down to the beach. We won't swim until your papa joins us, but we can splash in the little waves.'

Louis tore off his pyjamas and frisked round her, his small body brown as a berry apart from the white triangle where his bathing trunks had protected him from the sun.

'I could wake Papa, only I think he's already getting up, I heard a swore from his room a little while ago.'

'A swear, not a swore. In that case, hurry, and we'll get our swim before breakfast.'

'All right.' Deborah stepped into the shower and turned on the water even as a small voice said plaintively, outside the door, 'If we're going to bathe, mademoiselle, why must I wash?'

'No arguing, just wash!'

'I *am*, mademoiselle! I only *asked*!'

Presently, ths two of them descended the stairs

and went into the kitchen, where Suzanne, singing, was baking bread. She turned as they entered, smiling.

'Early birds, eh? But not so early as Monsieur Frenaye! He left a few minutes ago, rushing off somewhere in the car. Not a bite to eat either. But he said he'd be having breakfast with Mrs Brightmore, so if you'd like yours now, you're welcome.'

Abruptly, the sunshine left the morning. There was an aching void somewhere round Deborah's heart which resolutely refused to be comforted by the fact that she had known he was going off before breakfast to see Renata. She had forgotten, that was all. But in any case, she felt that in view of what had happened last night, he should have telephoned Renata and told her he would be unable to join her. He owed it to her, Deborah, to be here, in case Louis asked awkward questions. He was not to know that the child had completely forgotten his 'dream'.

She glanced at Louis and saw her disappointment mirrored in the small face. She patted his shoulder.

'Oh dear, I'm sorry, mon vieux, papa did tell me last night that he was seeing Renata this morning for breakfast. I'm afraid I forgot. What shall we do? Papa doesn't think I'm a good enough swimmer to take care of you and he's right, of course, so I shouldn't really take you down there by myself.'

Suzanne looked from one disappointed face to the other.

'Mr Tom bathes each morning,' she suggested diffidently. 'How about giving him a ring, asking him to come over to breakfast? He'd come like a shot, I'm sure.'

'I don't think we can do that, but I could ring him now and ask him if he could swim later.' Deborah volunteered. She walked to the kitchen doorway. 'What's his number, do you know?'

'It's in the address book,' Suzanne said. 'What do you want for breakfast today, Deborah?'

'Oh, I don't know. Orange juice and toast, I suppose.' And then, as Guy's desertion struck her anew, 'No, I'll have the same as Louis for once.'

Louis always had an English breakfast, and a great deal of that, too. It was the biggest meal he ate all day, and he did justice to it. Suzanne looked surprised.

'Bacon, scrambled eggs, tomatoes and beans. You *sure*, Deborah?'

'Why not? Shan't be a moment.'

She rang Tom Saunders, but he was unable to oblige her.

'Normally I'd come like a shot,' he assured her when she had outlined the plan. 'But Guy brought all his paperwork back with him, and I'm gradually working my through it. That's why I couldn't go to the Dumart's barbecue last night. Was it fun?'

'Not bad. Well, give me a ring when you get through the work, and perhaps you can come swimming with us then.'

'Great!' Tom's voice lifted. 'See you then, Deborah.'

'See you, Tom.'

Afterwards, grimly wading through her enormous breakfast out on the terrace, Deborah glowered round at the sunshine and the flowers and hated herself, Guy Frenaye and the island in equal proportions. He had walked into her bedroom last night, cast her down on the bed, made passionate love to her — and then promptly forgotten all about her. And she — she had let him. Not a knee in the groin, not a scratch nor a bite had she used in

96

self-defence. And as for the island! It was just like some wretched nineteen-thirties vamp, lying beneath the hot sun, sensuous and perfumed, encouraging behaviour such as his — and hers.

What we need is a spell of good, cold weather, she told herself. A nice hailstorm, now, that would take some of the bloom off the place, make it more down to earth! She bit into her toast so hard that a burnt crumb flew into her eye, making her jump and swear.

Then she laughed at herself and took a drink of orange juice. She was being absurd. The sun was warm, the sky was blue, and Guy had not meant to terrify his son. She, too, had been innocent of everything but thoughtlessness. However, she would make very sure that she never got into such a position again . . .

6

'I'm not being difficult, Guy, I just said I couldn't understand it, and I can't. Why should Renata completely and utterly ignore Louis for weeks, not make one single effort to see him, and then suddenly, out of the blue, say she wants to take him out? And why must it be this afternoon, when Tom and I were going to take him into Castlebridge for another wander round the animal market? Tom's got the afternoon off, and we were going for a swim later, and Suzanne was doing us a picnic, and we were — '

'What does it matter whether Saunders has time off or not?' Guy's blue eyes were cold. 'There's a bus, or I could have given you a lift any day if you'd said you wanted to visit the market.'

'I daresay. The point is that it was all arranged, and Louis was looking forward to it. He doesn't understand it any more than I do, but he does know he's being done out of a treat and given an undeserved punishment instead.'

'Punishment? So you've encouraged the boy to regard Renata's company as punishment! That is not what I employed you to do, mademoiselle.'

It was breakfast time, and the two of them were on the terrace, the table between them. The meal was over, but both had a cup of rapidly cooling coffee before them, destined to be ignored whilst their battle raged.

'What nonsense, monsieur! Renata's treatment of Louis has been enough to give him a dislike of her. When she sees the boy in company, what does she do? She seizes his chin, gets covered in ice-cream, and makes a fuss, telling half the world that he's dirty, a ragamuffin. And before I came to the island he disliked her, so please don't try to blame *me* for your son's antipathy towards Renata! Anyway, in view of the way she treats him, it's an understandable dislike.'

'There's nothing understandable about it. Renata's done her best to make friends with the boy, she's — '

'Done her best! When, may I ask? I've been here for — '

'Don't start that all over again!' They were both on their feet now, both glaring. 'I employ you, mademoiselle, to do as I tell you, not to query my every order. Get Louis ready after lunch and Renata will take him off your hands for the afternoon. I'm sure Saunders will be happy to have you to himself for a change. So you see, there's one advantage in Renata's offer. It will allow you to enjoy Tom's company for once!'

Deborah's hands flew to her hips and she opened her mouth to tell Guy that she would enjoy Tom's company a great deal more than she enjoyed his. Then she closed her lips, tightly. Exercising all the self-control at her command she sat down again, and reached for her half-empty coffee cup.

'Very well, monsieur.'

He sat down too, eyeing her smoulderingly across the table.

'My God, woman, you're impossible sometimes!

Renata's not been in touch because she didn't want to spoil the excellent relationship you were building up with the boy. You do know *why* we keep flying at each other's throats, I suppose?'

'Certainly I do. But I've no wish to insult you any further today by telling you!'

He gave a short bark of laughter, then reached across and took her hands, tightly clasped and lying on the table.

'It's because you won't be natural with me, and you won't let me be natural with you. Damn it, I only want — '

'I know what you want, monsieur, and it isn't what I want! Now could we change the subject, please?'

'Damn it, no!' He banged his fist violently on the table, making their coffee cups jump. 'Anyone would think I was some sex fiend, the way you behave! If I brush your fingers with mine you snatch back your hand as if I had the plague; if I touch you in the water whilst we're bathing, you're halfway up the beach and dragging a towel over you before I can take a breath. Damn it, do you think you're irresistible? Because you aren't! You're just — '

'And neither are you! You may not be a sex fiend, but you think you've got a right to try to make love to me, and I'm not in the market for a shabby little affair with my employer!' They had both leapt to their feet again, their faces reddening, their bodies tense with fury. 'Just leave me alone and forget that you're an irresistible and sexy Frenchman, because that cuts no ice with me!'

'Oh, is that so? You think you're so cool, so collected . . . ' Hard hands shot out and caught her shoulders in a painful grip. He half dragged her across the table, shaking her as he did so until the long, fine blonde hair fell concealingly across her face and he could only see the soft scarlet of her underlip, the rounded chin. 'By God, but I'd like to have the schooling of you, you self-opinionated, prim little English virgin! If there's one thing I can't stand — '

'Papa, why must I go with Aunt Renata this afternoon?' Louis appeared in the French windows, a scowl marring his brow. 'Deborah said we could go to the animal market in the town, and I do so love the animal market! And Tom said we'd have tea, like last time, only at an even better place. Couldn't we — '

'NO WE COULD NOT!' Guy's roar of annoyance was so loud that Louis blinked and fell back a step. 'You're going to have a lovely time with your Aunt Renata and don't forget it. Now go up and fetch your towel and we'll go for a swim.'

Deborah, who had been abruptly released at the sound of Louis's voice, put her hair back from her face with shaking hands. Tears were not far away but she did not intend to shed them in front of Guy. He should not see how upset she was, should not count it as another victory. She moved towards the house.

'I'll get my towel too. Shan't be long.'

She and Louis went upstairs, then she put on her bathing suit, took a big towel from the shower cubicle, and accompanied the still grumbling Louis downstairs.

'Don't fuss, mon brave, you'll only annoy papa,' she advised him, but he continued to tell the world in a shrill treble that he had no desire to go on an outing with his Aunt Renata. In desperation, Deborah tried a small bribe. 'Look, we'll go to the animal market tomorrow, even if we catch the bus.

This isn't *instead* of your treat, it's an *extra* treat.'

'Huh!' Louis said succinctly, but at that moment they emerged on to the terrace once more and his father's grim expression was enough to keep Louis quiet for a while.

Inevitably, the bathe was not a success. Guy ignored Deborah and swam further out than she cared to go, for though her swimming was improving daily she still did not like being right out of her depth. And Louis was aggressive and difficult in a way Deborah had never seen him. He kicked over her towel, threw himself down in a tiny pool and swore in French patois when she chided him, and then, when she announced that they had best return to the house, had a tantrum.

'You see?' Guy said, picking his son up and slapping his bottom until the shrieks subsided into sobs. 'He knows you disapprove of this outing, so he's showing whose side he's on.'

'Rubbish!' Deborah glared at Guy as he stood Louis down with a thump on the sand. 'He's distressed because he's dreading it and thinks it will be back to where he was before I came.' She rumpled Louis's hair lovingly. 'He's so seldom naughty, you didn't have to whack him like that!'

'I won't stand for him being rude to anyone. What is this, anyway, a tug of love?' He glanced out to sea, speaking stiffly, with his back half turned to her. 'I happen to be very fond of the little blighter, in my way.'

'I know. I'm sorry.' Deborah knelt down beside Louis. 'Darling, papa and I are getting upset because you're upset and that will never do, will it? So would you make the best of this afternoon, mon vieux? And now let's go and visit Essie and get her to make us a nice cup of tea. Papa's got lots of work to do this morning, I'm sure.'

There was a short pause, during which Louis looked uncertainly from Deborah to his father and back again. He was waiting, she realised, for Guy to voice some sort of disapproval of Essie. And then, when Guy merely grinned at them, the little boy hurled himself at Guy's knees.

'I'm sorry I was naughty, Papa. Come with us, and I'll show you how Prince Charles begs for a biscuit.'

But even the prospect of such a rare treat could not sway Guy from his determination to do some work, so they parted, Deborah to slip into her towelling robe and accompany Louis to Essie's cottage, and Monsieur Frenaye to make his own plans.

Their welcome at the cottage was predictably warm. Prince Charles, ears flying, came rushing to meet them, and Essie had the kettle simmering on the hob before they had even set foot in her kitchen.

'I see my boy's been cryin',' she remarked, giving Louis a big hug. 'Jest 'cos Miz Brightmore's takin' you out fer a while? That ain't nothin' to cry about, she give you good time, I guess.'

'How did you know, Essie?' Deborah said curiously, pouring milk into the fine china cups in their daily ritual. 'She didn't ring until quite late last night, I don't think.'

'I tell you. Louis, go get Prince Charles a biscuit from the tin with a picture of ole King George on it. Right?'

'Right,' echoed Louis cheerfully. Now that he was in Essie's company all his annoyance over the afternoon seemed to have dissipated. 'We're going to the animal market tomorrow, Deborah says.

There are puppies there, and monkeys, and guinea pigs, and . . . Hey, Prince Charles, don't knock me over, or I shan't be able to get you your biscuit!'

'Go on, Essie, how did you know?' Deborah said as soon as Louis was busy in the little lean-to she referred to as her kitchen. 'Have you been up to Frèremaison already this morning?'

Essie chuckled but shook her head.

'Naw! I knowed last night, Deb'rah, soon's Miz Brightmore made up her mind. Before Monsieur Guy did, very like. My son Ceddie's a waiter at the hotel where Miz Brightmore lives. Seems dey's a feller stayin' there with a boy, must be a year or two older dan our Louis. Wanted to ask his boy up to see dat ole volcano, so Miz Brightmore, she ups and says she's got a nephew near 'nuff the same age as his boy. An' thass how it wuz arranged.'

'Oh, they're going up to see Old Gasper, are they? Well, Louis should enjoy that, don't you think?'

Essie looked doubtful.

'I dunno, Deb'rah. Trouble is, Louis don't ever see no other chillun so he ain't used to boys, and he ain't fond o' Miz Brightmore. Is Monsieur Guy goin' along?'

'I don't know, but I shouldn't think so. He didn't mention it, at any rate. But Mr Guy and I aren't on terribly good terms at the moment. I didn't want to send Louis off with Mrs Brightmore, but his father couldn't see my point. So we quarrelled.'

'Hm. He shout at you, eh?' Essie's face took on a dreamy, far-away look. 'I could give you sumpin' to mek him sweet's sugar candy to you, if you like.'

'And what might that be?' Deborah stared suspiciously at the seamed old face. 'If it's what I think it is, no thanks; Monsieur Frenaye doesn't need that sort of encouragement! In fact we'd probably get on a good deal better if he wasn't so . . . well, if he didn't . . . Well, no thanks.'

Essie grinned triumphantly.

'I thought so! He'm already thataway over you, hey, Deb'rah? Why won't you let things tek their course?'

'Because I'm not like that,' Deborah said firmly. 'The world, dear Essie, is not well lost for love. Well, perhaps it is for love, but not just for giving in to every handsome man who kisses you! I'm here to do a job of work, to teach Louis English and to look after him, and that's all I intend to do. So don't you go slipping anything into my tea, there's a dear!'

The bright old eyes regarded her shrewdly for a moment, then Essie chuckled again and shook her grey curls.

'No need, Deb'rah. No need. I kin see it's already there, ain't it? That feelin', the warm feelin' that won't go away, no matter how he shout, no matter how you weep!' She sighed gustily and with relish. 'I wuz young onçe, Deb'rah, I know well how it feels.'

'Do you indeed, Essie? Would you like another cup of tea?'

'An' you ache to deny him, ain't that right, gal? Ache and ache, in de breasts, de shoulders, de hips, de thighs! Why don' you give in an' enjoy life?'

Deborah drained her tea, then got to her feet.

'Just because something's difficult, that doesn't make it wrong, you know, Essie! I've other friends, good ones, here as well. There's Tom, and the American, Travers, and . . . '

'Them!' There was a world of contempt in her tone. 'Only one brings the feelin', gal!'

'Well, I don't know that you're right about that.'

She walked over to the doorway. 'Come along, mon vieux, we've got work to do at Frèremaison.' She turned to face Essie once more. 'You're a wicked old woman, do you know that? I've already told you that I don't believe in all this free love and sleeping around. I believe in the old-fashioned things like marriage, and one man one woman until death do them part. See?'

'I sho' do see, Deb'rah. Monsieur Guy felt like that once, else he'd never ha . . . ' Louis entered the room at a trot. 'Am you ready to go, Louis? Give ole Essie a kiss!'

As they left, she waddled across to the door and put her old head near Deborah's.

'Give him a chance, gal! Let him git close, an' warm, an' mebbe he'll surprise you.'

'Huh!' Deborah said, echoing Louis. But as the two of them made their way back to Frèremaison she could not help wondering about what Essie had said. Had his first marriage soured his attitude to women? And what exactly did Essie mean when she said that Guy might surprise her? Could it be that he, too, would want to marry the woman he loved? She was pretty sure that he would not wish to marry the one he merely seduced, however.

She acknowledged, ruefully, that there was a lot of truth in Essie's other pronouncements. Her feelings for Guy Frenaye were complicated, but they did not alter. She was still annoyed with him, there were moments when she hated him, yet beneath it all, colouring everything he did or said, was that warmth. Even when he was most furious with her, when she knew his fingers itched to slap her, and when she, for two pins, would have retaliated every bit as fiercely, the warmth for him burned within her, a steady flame of feeling.

'How long shall I be away, mademoiselle? Will Aunt Renata make me have tea with her?'

Deborah's heart smote her. Here was she, thinking of nothing but herself and her own problems, and poor Louis was facing an ordeal with which, at five years old, he was ill-equipped to deal.

'Look, petit chou, I've had an idea! How would it be if we came to the same place that Auntie's taking you to? Then we can have a little wave and a little smile when no one's looking. And it can seem like an accidental meeting. How would that be?'

His face brightened at once. A smile dawned and the small hand within her own squeezed her fingers ecstatically.

'Oh, mademoiselle!'

'Is it a bargain, then? You'll be very good for Auntie Renata, and Tom and I will do our best to join you some time during the afternoon.'

He nodded hard, then broke away from her to gambol ahead. His voice rose in song.

'Nelly the elephant packed her tronk . . . '

'Her trunk, darling.'

'That's what I said. Tronk!' He turned to smile at her and Deborah smiled back. Surely Tom, who was so obliging, would not object to taking her to see Old Gasper, as the volcano was nicknamed by the locals? It was extinct, of course, but it still had hot streams and ash and things, she believed. They had intended to swim and it might be possible to do that, but probably, since they were to be spared the animal market until the next day, Tom would prefer to do something a little more sophisticated. His attentions had become very marked lately, and this would be their first daytime outing alone together. In fact, now that she thought about it, it would be their first outing together, for though Guy said he was quite agreeable to her going out in the evenings, it had never been convenient when she mentioned that Tom wanted to take her somewhere.

Fortunately, perhaps, Guy was so furious with her than even the thought of her and Tom going off alone somewhere had not deterred him. He had practically ordered her to enjoy Tom's company, and she would do so! She ran to catch Louis up, breaking into defiant song.

'Off she went with a trompety tromp . . . '

*   *   *

'Are you ready, Louis?' Guy stood in the bedroom doorway, immaculate in a pale blue silk shirt and dark slacks. He had a pair of dark glasses in one hand and some binoculars slung round his neck but he was not, it transpired, going to visit the volcano with his son. Hs was merely going to lend the binoculars to Renata. 'I told Auntie I'd deliver you to her hotel by two, so don't be long.'

Louis straightened his shoulders, gave Deborah one last desperate look, and marched over to his father. He was obeying orders to make the best of it and had, indeed, been quite intrigued to learn that there would be another boy present and one, moreover, who might well play with him.

'Au revoir, mon brave,' Deborah said gently. 'Don't forget to look around you and notice things, and if Auntie takes you out to tea, try not to dribble icecream.'

'Au revoir, mademoiselle.' Louis took his father's hand. He looked very small in his white shirt and dark blue shorts, very small and neat and foreign all of a sudden and quite different from the happy little boy in the faded shorts and T-shirts who usually roamed Frèremaison. 'I will be good. See you later.'

Deborah ran to the window and waved until the car was out of sight, then returned to her room to prepare for her own afternoon out. It was very warm, and since she intended to persuade Tom to take her to visit the volcano she put on a yellow silk shirt and matching shorts, slinging a full skirt into her bag just in case they stayed out late and the evening grew cooler. She considered her bathing suit, then decided against taking it. The volcano was inland, and she had long wanted to see some hut circles not too far distant. They could do both, perhaps, and then return to Castlebridge for after-noon tea, but it was unlikely that they would find time to bathe.

When the car horn sounded outside the front door she was ready, her belongings in her big straw bag, her dark glasses pushed up into her hair. She ran out of the house and across the drive, then stopped short, her hand on the car door.

'What on earth . . . ?'

'Get in. I'll explain as we go.'

It was Guy, looking grim. Her heart missed a beat. She scrambled into the passenger seat.

'What's wrong? Is it Louis? Has something happened?'

'Not as far as I know. I left him with Renata, looking quite happy. But Tom's . . . busy this afternoon, and couldn't get away. So I said I'd take you wherever you wanted to go. Into Castlebridge, and then out for a picnic, that's what Tom had in mind, I believe, or was it the other way round?'

'Busy? But he said he was off this afternoon. He said he'd caught up . . . he could have rung me!'

'Why should he? I said I'd explain.'

'Well, I suppose . . . only I had planned . . . Look, could you do the explaining whilst I think?'

He glanced sideways at her.

'I found that one of the plantations hadn't handed in the right figures. I told Tom that tomorrow would do, but then I remembered you'd promised Louis a trip into Castlebridge tomorrow, so I told Tom and he said he'd do the stuff this afternoon.'

He sounded infuriatingly pleased with himself.

'Oh, I see. Well, since you can't possibly take me where I'd planned to go, and Tom plainly can't either, perhaps you could drop me off at Trav's place? He'll be very — '

His foot went down on the accelerator and the car roared forward. Deborah shut her eyes as a corner was rounded far too fast and apparently with the use of only two wheels.

'My God, Guy, are you trying to kill us both? You must be mad!'

'I *am* mad, though not in the sense you mean. I am taking you out for the afternoon, not some half-baked youngster with a crew-cut and bedroom eyes!' He ground the words out through gritted teeth and she sighed and sat back, wondering why he should say such things about Travers, whom he scarcely knew.

'All right, it was only a suggestion.' She used her calmest and most peaceable tone. 'But I did have plans for this afternoon, and I know they're plans that you'll disapprove of. Only a promise is a promise, and . . . oh, dear!'

He skidded the car to a halt at the roadside and switched off the engine, then turned towards her. He stared at her, his brows almost meeting above his nose. She could see a small muscle jumping at the side of his mouth.

'Well? Just exactly what had you planned that I wouldn't approve of? The truth, if you please!'

'I thought Tom and I could visit the volcano. I've never been, and when Essie told me that Renata was taking Louis there, I thought . . . I thought . . . '

'You thought you'd interfere, break into their afternoon.' His voice was heavy with sarcasm. 'For crying out loud, woman, this is an honest attempt to allow Renata and the boy to get to know one another! Don't you see, the mere sight of you might well make Louis feel homesick, lost. He'd want to join you, be unable to do so . . . well, it's out of the question, anyway. I've got other plans.'

'You may be right. But I told Louis I'd be there, so I have to go!'

He stared at her for a moment and then, slowly, he shook his head. His eyes flickered over her, an almost insulting approval in their depths.

'No. You'll go where I take you, mademoiselle! And I intend to take you somewhere quiet, where we can talk, swim perhaps, lie in the sun. It's time that you and I, also, got to know one another.'

A shiver shook her. She tried to disguise it, reaching up to pat her hair into place, but she feared that he had both seen and understood. The thought of being alone with him, getting to know him, was not repugnant to her. It sent shivers through her, made the soft hair on the nape of her neck prickle with guilty excitement. But it would never do to admit it. She turned to face him, and laid a pleading hand on his tanned, muscular arm.

'Please, Guy, I couldn't bear to let Louis down! Please take me to the volcano, if only for a few moments, just so that I can give him a wave and a smile. Afterwards, I'll go wherever you want, if you'll only let me keep my promise first.'

'No. It was a promise you had no right to give.' He leaned forward and turned on the engine. 'Don't you see that to turn up there is to destroy the whole purpose of the exercise?'

'Oh, monsieur, don't *you* see that to break one's word to a little boy is a dreadful thing, especially to a little boy who is as — as anxious as Louis?'

He drove forward, then gunned the big car down the road, not taking his eyes from the tarmac in front of them.

'I do not. Now we'll forget the whole subject, please. I'm taking you to a tiny bay where I keep a boat. I brought a picnic . . . ' he jerked his head at the back seat and, glancing over her shoulder, Deborah saw the picnic basket, ' . . . and some wine. Renata's taking the boy to her hotel for dinner, and will bring him back and help Suzanne to put him to bed. So we should be able to have a very pleasant outing, if you'll just relax for once.'

Deborah found that she was trembling. She could tell herself that Louis would understand, would realise that she had been unable to join him, but nothing could rid her of the fear that he would never trust her word again. Worse, that he might blame his father too, so that the two largest influences in his childish world would suddenly become frail reeds which could not be relied on. It would send him back to Essie, make him moody again, give him a distaste for the English nation as a whole . . . the list went on and on, getting progressively blacker in her imagination.

However, she was beginning to know Guy as well as his son. If she persisted in begging him to take her to the volcano, he would merely lose his temper and convince himself that she was being difficult. She must play her hand more cunningly than that, and perhaps she might get to the volcano after all.

'Is it far to this bay, Guy?'

'Not far now.'

'I wish I'd known! I didn't bring a bikini because I thought we'd be inland.'

He grunted, then flicked his indicator and swerved the big car round a tight corner. Ahead of her, Deborah could see palm trees and behind them, the curve of a small, silver-sanded bay and the brilliant blue of the sea. Guy drew the car to a halt in a scatter of sand, then got out and walked round to open her door.

'Out with you!'

She climbed out and surveyed the scene. It was an enchanted spot, the beach deserted, the sea breaking in tiny ripples on the shore. Big outcrops of rock cast patches of deep shade on the sand and the palms moved their leaves in the sea breeze. It was very quiet. Barely a sound broke the silence save for the soft hushing of the sea.

'Like it?'

'It's beautiful.' She took the hand he held out to her and they walked across the beach to one of the rocky outcrops. In its shade, he set down the picnic basket and his own bag. Then he began to take off his slacks. He was wearing bathing trunks underneath them, to Deborah's considerable relief. Nude bathing in such a secluded spot might be perfectly safe in one sense, but it was not at all safe in another!

'I'm going in. It's too hot to sunbathe unless you've cooled off first. Care to join me?'

She pulled a wry face and settled herself on the shaded sand.

114

'How can I?'

He sat down beside her, then put a casual arm round her shoulder.

'Don't Englishwomen wear bras and briefs? You'll soon dry off in this heat, and I doubt they will horrify the seabirds.'

'That's true — that we wear them, I mean. I suppose . . . ' She sighed. 'Oh dear, I'm a mass of inhibitions, aren't I? All right!'

He took his arm off her shoulders and turned to gaze at her, one eyebrow lifting quizzically.

'You mean you will bathe? My powers of persuasion must be improving.'

'Or perhaps my powers of resistance are crumbling.' She knew it was a foolish thing to say as soon as it was out of her mouth, but what had been said could not be unsaid. She glanced apprehensively at him and was betrayed, by his expression, into a giggle. 'Sorry, sorry! Turn your back would you?'

He grinned at her but obediently turned his back, addressing her over his shoulder.

'Why, for God's sake, when the moment you've done the deed we shall run down to the sea together.'

'I told you I was full of inhibitions. Once I'm undressed I shall tell myself I'm wearing a white bikini and probably manage to convince myself that what I'm doing is perfectly proper. Until then, I shall feel slightly sinful. See?'

She took off her shirt, shorts and sandals, then glanced down at herself. The white lacy bra could have been a rather inadequate bikini top, the briefs were quite a respectable bikini bottom. She touched his bronzed shoulder lightly.

'I'm ready.'

He turned and his eyes took her in from top to toe; the expression in their depths was one of admiration, though the beginning of a smile did tug at his lips.

'*Very* nice! Now, cherie, let's cool it!' He took her hand and they ran down to the sea and plunged simultaneously into the delicious coolness of the waves. Shoulder to shoulder they swam out until he turned to her, stood up, and put his arms lightly round her.

'Good to be cool?' He kissed her, his lips gentle, experimental almost. As different from . . . she pushed the thought of Guy's other kisses out of her mind. This was Guy trying to mend their differences and begin a good relationship, she reminded herself. And so I can respond, though definitely not with too much ardour!

He was first to break the kiss, suggesting that they swim out a little further to where a small reef would attract marine life. Deborah was doubtful. Though her swimming had improved, it was still nowhere near as strong as Guy's.

'We-ell, I'd like to see the fish and the coral and everything, but is it very deep? I'm not terribly good yet, and suppose there were octupuses?'

He grinned.

'I shan't let you drown. I've other fates in store for you! Come on!'

She almost forgot her anxiety about Louis as they swam over the reef, but soon enough Guy decided they must return to the shore.

'The sun's hot out here, ma petite, and you've no oil on your shoulders and back. We'll do our sunbathing ashore, I think.'

They returned to the beach and walked up it towards their clothes. He held her hand, their fingers linked. His touch, as always, brought the warmth that Essie had mentioned. A glow, a comfortable feeling, no more than that. But good, seeming to tell her that it was right to be with him, to touch him.

Reaching their camp, Guy spread out his towel, for Deborah had none, and they lay side by side on it, on their stomachs. They were so close that she could feel the warmth emanating from his skin, see the water on him diamond beaded on each dark hair.

'Don't fall asleep, Deborah, or I'll have to wake you to turn over in ten minutes.'

Deborah snorted. Was it likely that she would fall asleep, in her underwear, with him so close? She shot a glance at him, and saw that he had read her thoughts and was amused by them.

'I'm on my best behaviour today, ma jeaune fille! Bake away for ten minutes, then.'

She obeyed, then turned after ten minutes and baked her front. But after that he sat up, shook himself, and tossed her shirt across her tummy.

'My skin's like leather but yours isn't, thank the Lord, so cover up now, chérie, and I'll get the wine. I left it in the boot.'

Whilst he was gone she examined her wristwatch. Renata and Louis would be at the volcano now, and the time had come for her next move. She was oddly reluctant to make it, though. He was being so marvellous, so gentle and natural! She might succeed, of course, but suppose she just ruined everything?

He returned, sat down beside her and reaching for the hamper, opened it.

'There, hasn't Suzanne done us proud? There's nothing forgotten, I bet. How about starting with some cold chicken, home-made rolls, and salad?'

She had her shirt on now, tied beneath her breasts so that her midriff could still feel the air but her shoulders were protected from the sun. She fiddled with the knot, her eyes cast down.

'No thanks, Guy. I'm not hungry.'

He stopped moving, ferreting in the basket. She sensed that he was staring at her.

'Not hungry?'

'That's right.'

'Oh! How about a glass of wine, then? Or I could brew some tea, if you'd like that.'

She shook her head, though it went to her heart to do so. She could have drunk forty cups of tea.

His shadow fell on her. It was cool across her face and shoulders as he stood, looking down at her.

'Deborah, are you about to be a spoil-sport?'

She looked at him apprehensively. He did not look angry, but resigned and bitter. He was pushing the cork back into the bottle with unnecessary thoroughness.

'I see. I understand. But if you insist on my taking you to see Old Gasper it's the last time I try to put us back on a friendly and informal footing. If you insist, then I'm your employer and nothing more.'

Deborah got slowly to her feet. She held his eyes, her own pleading.

'Guy, you don't know how wretched you make me feel, but I gave my word! I can't let him down, and I don't believe, in your heart, you'd like me very much if I did.'

He shrugged, then turned towards the car.

'We are to go, then?' And, at her nod, 'Get dressed.'

She obeyed like lightning, but with a sad and heavy heart.

118

7

Once on the road leading to the volcano, Deborah simply sat beside Guy and hated her own thoughtlessness and stupidity. Guy would never forgive her, never again be an affectionate companion, a friend who might become more than a friend. And what was more, he was quite right. Sympathy for Louis's plight had led her to plan what she now acknowledged was an intrusion. Renata should have been given the chance to make her peace with her nephew. Even Essie, who was prejudiced against Renata with good cause, had seen that. But had she? No! All she had seen was a frightened little boy, and her own crusading spirit had done the rest.

On the other hand, she had felt strongly that Louis would be one against three in the company of Renata and her friends. He had never met Renata's pal, Edmund Cruckshank, nor Edmund's son Raymond, and all he knew of his aunt was that he disliked her. It would have been lovely, of course, to think that Louis and Raymond would like one another on sight, but Deborah was a realist. Because Louis never met other children he had no natural, easy manners with them. She had seen him when they went round the animal market or the shops, eyeing other children with as much nervous interest as though he thought that they, too, should

119

be behind bars. She had mentioned it to Guy but he had not seemed particularly interested, save to remark that the boy would have his fill of his peers when he started school.

As they neared the place, however, she found her anxiety for Louis replacing all other emotions so that she gripped her hands together until the nails tore the flesh, and felt rivulets of sweat course down between her breasts. It no longer mattered that she had injured her relationship with Guy; that was not irremediable; surely he could be won round? But if something *had* happened to Louis, if he had trusted to her presence to save him from a situation with which he could not deal, then she would never forgive herself.

'We can park the car here, as most people do, or I can drive right up.'

Guy's voice cut across her thoughts, and she heard that his tone was harsh with impatience but scarcely cared, for now a conviction that all was not well with Louis was growing within her, dark, terrible.

'Drive up, please,' she said breathlessly. She was leaning forward in her seat, trying to propel the car forward by her will, anxious for the first sight of the crater of Old Gasper. 'Guy, I have this feeling . . .'

He clashed the gears, beginning to crawl up the steep incline, no doubt thinking that she had not heard his rude remark about superstitious little fools, but she scarcely heeded it. She must, she *must* find Louis!

The moment the car stopped she jumped out and hurried over to where crowds of tourists were gathered, all looking in the same direction. They were happy, eating icecreams, calling out to each other. Guy, who had followed her, caught her arm.

'Well? Have you seen him? Can we leave?'

'No, and I don't think they're here. Guy, she *said* she'd bring him here. What can have happened to make her change her mind? They can't have left already, surely?'

He tugged at her arm, turning her, leading her back towards the car.

'Calm yourself, girl, nothing's happened; they've just gone down a little earlier. Maybe one of the boys got bored, said he'd prefer a bathe, or a decent tea in Castlebridge.' He patted her shoulder. 'Look, I did as you asked. I brought you here, though I was sure it was foolishness. Can we go now? I'd like to salvage something of my afternoon.'

But her premonition, if it could be dignified by such a name, could not be ignored, told to go away. She wrenched herself out of his hold and turned, running back to where a group of tourists were being lectured by a tall, thin guide with a sunhat perched on the back of his curly black hair.

'Excuse me. Can you tell me if you've seen a little boy in navy shorts and a white shirt, with a very striking, red-haired lady?'

Behind her, she heard Guy mutter something about going too far, accosting strangers with unlikely questions, but she paid no heed. The man was frowning down at her.

'You the mother? That kid sure was in a poor way, ma'am! He's bin taken down to Castlebridge Hospital; left no more than fifteen, twenty minutes since. They'll take good care of him, ma'am.'

Deborah's hand flew to her heart and the breath stopped in her throat. She could not say the words which fought to escape, but Guy said them for her.

'What happened?'

His voice was harsh with shock.

'The redhead had two lads with her, one must've been ten, the littl'un, the one who fell, around four or five. The big 'un was teasing, fooling around, pretending to push the littl'un. And when auntie called that she was going to buy icecreams, and whoever reached her first could choose the flavour, the big boy, he kinda turned on the other one. The kid was scared, I guess. He stepped back, didn't realise the lip of the crater was so near.'

She heard Guy's breath rasp in his throat.

'My God! And fell?'

'That's right. On to a ledge, mind, but he was unconscious when they brought him up. They took him off at once, the three of 'em. The big lad was blubbing, trying to touch the littl'un.' He turned back to Deborah once more. 'You his mother, lady? He sure wanted his mom. Called for her as he tipped over. *Mudder, mudder*, he shouted.'

Deborah turned blindly away. He had not called for his mother, but for mademoiselle, who had promised to be there, promised to keep him safe! Tears blurred her eyes, but she hurried back the way they had come, heading for the car as fast as she could over the rough terrain. Close by her, she knew it without having to glance at him, Guy strode. He would take her to the hospital and they would find out what happened and what harm had been done.

The car was unlocked and they jumped in almost simultaneously. Without even pausing for her to strap herself in, Guy started the engine and began the journey back into Castlebridge.

They were travelling a good deal faster than was safe, Deborah realised, before they had been on the road two minutes. But this time she did not care.

This time, all she wanted was to get to Louis, to be with him, hold his hand, tell him that she *had* gone to the volcano, but had arrived there too late.

It seemed hours later that they screeched to a halt before the hospital entrance, but it could only have been a few minutes. They both jumped out of the car and ran, side by side, into the foyer. It was crowded, but they ignored the patients waiting and made straight for the reception desk. Deborah, her mouth dry, began to stammer out the question they longed to ask, but Guy caught hold of her hand and squeezed it, quieting her.

'Hush, Deb.' He turned to the nursing sister, who was eyeing them curiously. 'My son, Sister — Louis Frenaye — is he here?'

A big ledger lay on the desk. The nurse opened it and ran a finger down the page.

'What was he in for, sir? This is outpatients, we deal with accidents and emergencies, but not with normal admissions.'

'He had a fall. He was up at the Old Gasper.'

'Oh, yes, I remember. His aunt and uncle brought him in, I believe. He's been admitted to the children's ward. I'll get someone to take you up there.' She called a passing nurse in a rather pretty pink uniform over. 'Louis Frenaye's parents, Nurse. Would you take them along to the children's ward, please?'

'Certainly, Sister.' The younger woman turned to them. 'It's this way.'

The children's ward was brightly decorated with wide windows, air conditioning, and murals on the walls, but Deborah noticed only the children, dressing gowned, cheerful, pattering around the beds, and the staff moving amongst them. She looked anxiously round. Where was Louis? But the sister in charge soon put a stop to her wondering. Louis was in a side ward.

'He was concussed, though he has come round and is sleeping now. He has a broken tibia, but it's a straightforward fracture, which shouldn't give too much trouble.' Her bright, professional smile swept them both. 'I've left a student nurse watching him since his aunt went rushing off, presumably to find you, but if you'd like to take over from her, it would be much more satisfactory He doesn't know us, so it's difficult for us to judge whether he's rambling or making good sense.'

'Of course.' Deborah tried to smile back but it was a poor effort. 'Can we go to him at once?'

'Certainly, Mother.' Deborah blinked. Mother? 'Come with me.'

They followed her along the corridor but at the door of Louis's side ward she stopped for a moment.

'Very quiet, if you please. He had a nasty bump on the head, he needs his sleep.'

They entered the small room. Air conditioning buzzed and the blinds were drawn, filtering the bright sunshine. Louis lay, unnaturally neat and still, in the centre of the small bed. He looked drawn and wizened, a tiny monkey. Deborah caught her breath on a sob and bent over him. His eyes were dark-circled and his mouth was open, giving him a defence-less look which made her long to hug him, to remind him of her love. But she could do nothing of the sort, she must sit down quietly, and watch until he woke of his own accord.

The sister moved quietly across the room, pulling two chairs forward, indicating them with a nod, then slipping out of the room, taking the young student nurse with her. Deborah sat down and Guy followed suit.

They waited for Louis to wake.

*   *   *

'Deb-or-ah?'

His dark, weary eyes opened and fixed on her countenance, the expression in them misty and vague. He was barely awake, barely conscious. She was on her knees by the bed instantly, her fingers smoothing down his cheek.

'Yes, mon vieux?'

'Where's this?'

'It's the hospital. You're safe, chéri, but you have a poor leg and a bump on the head.'

'Am I?' Louis turned his head slowly, as if it weighed a ton. 'Where's Papa?'

'I'm here, mon brave.' Guy moved forward, into Louis's range of vision. His hand came out as if he could not resist touching Louis, and stroked the dark hair. 'Poor fellow, what a bump you had!'

Louis frowned, his soft brows drawing together.

'A bump?'

'Only a little one. You'll be all right in a day or so.' Deborah spoke quickly, anxious to reassure. 'Does your head hurt?'

The frown deepened.

'Yes. I hurt all over. Papa?'

'What is it, Louis?'

'That boy pushed me. I hate him! I won't let him come to see Prince Charles after all. Don't let him, Papa! Don't!'

His distress was painful to watch. His chest rose and fell quickly, his lips were trembling. Colour flooded his face and a tear rolled down his cheek. Guy moved to the door.

'Steady, mon brave.' He turned to Deborah.

'Look, I'll fetch Sister, he shouldn't get in a state. You'll stay?'

'Of course. I'm going to tell Louis a quiet little story.'

It was soon clear, however, that Louis was in no state to listen to a story, no matter how quiet. He began to whimper, gripping her hand, his distress growing as memory returned. He had seemed quite lucid but suddenly he changed, he was crying out that Raymond was in the room, Raymond was hurting Prince Charles, calling to Essie to help whilst he fought to escape from the sheets and then cried out that his head hurt terribly, that he was thirsty, wanted to bathe in the sea.

Sister came rustling in, took in the situation at a glance, and hurried out again. Guy came over to the bed, his expression strained and anxious.

'He's very ill, isn't he? Sister's gone to get a doctor.' He gripped Deborah's shoulder, his fingers digging in unconsciously, so that she winced. 'My God, the poor brat! If only I'd listened instead of riding roughshod over you.'

It was a measure of his fondness for Louis, Deborah realised, that he could take the guilt so squarely on his own shoulders. She reached up, stroking the hand that gripped her flesh so tightly, wanting to reassure him.

'That's all wrong, Guy. You were right to try to stop me going after Louis. It was just that in a way I know him better than you do, so I was afraid that trouble might arise from the very fact that he is fascinated by other children but doesn't understand them. That, and an overdose of feminine intuition which sent us scampering up to the Old Gasper, of course.'

'You know him better than I do; that's where the

trouble lay. If I'd spent more time with him . . . '

Voices were raised in the corridor outside, high heels clicked on the polished lino.

'It's the doctor, and . . . ' Deborah was beginning, when the door burst open and Renata hurried into the room. Her face was streaked with tears, her mascara had run, her hair was wildly untidy. She glanced at Louis, then threw herself at Guy.

'My God, Guy, I've hunted everywhere for you! The poor lamb! I've felt so guilty, but we did what we could, we rushed him in here and then searched for you. That stupid, thoughtless Raymond, I could have killed him!' She turned to the bed, her glance resting properly on Louis's flushed and pain-racked countenance. 'My poor baby, and I meant to give you such a lovely treat!'

Guy's arms had gone round her instinctively, it seemed. Now he turned her gently towards the door as Louis began to whimper.

'He'll be all right, but he's a bit disturbed now, we're waiting for the doctor,' he said gently. 'Come along, I'll take you to Sister, she'll reassure you. Come along.'

They left the room and the door shut behind them. Deborah, who had risen to her feet, sat down on her chair and fixed her eyes on Louis's face. Poor baby, it was he who mattered, not Renata, not even Guy. She would stay with him as long as they would let her, but it did seem hard that Guy's presence and comfort should go to the woman who had caused the accident, and be denied to his son and herself.

However, he would not be long. He would return Renata to her hotel, perhaps, and then come back to them.

The door opening brought her hopes up, but it was only the doctor, a slim, serious looking young man, and a nurse. He smiled at Deborah and held out his hand.

'Mrs Frenaye? I'm Dr Milwall. I'll just take a look at your son, if you wouldn't mind waiting outside for a moment?'

'Of course not.' Deborah did not feel this was the time to tell anyone that she was not Louis's mother. She stood outside in the corridor for a very long ten minutes, and then the doctor joined her.

'I've given the child an injection to help him to sleep,' he told Deborah. 'He's very distressed by what happened, but children have remarkable powers of recovery. By morning he'll be boasting about his fall and demanding that everyone autographs his plaster.' He hesitated, glancing diffidently at her. 'Forgive me, but Nurse mentioned that Louis's parents are divorced, and I wondered . . .'

'Oh, I'm sorry, I should have told you just now that I'm Louis's nanny. I'm afraid I'm the nearest mother-substitute he has, he doesn't remember his own mother. His aunt . . . well, she was so distressed that Monsieur Frenaye has taken her home.'

'I see. He's fond of you, the boy?'

'I think so. I'm very fond of him!' She smiled at the doctor. 'My name's Deborah Barnett, by the way.'

'Ah! Would it be possible, Miss Barnett, for you to remain with him, just until he's over the worst? I believe he's French-speaking, and it can be very distressing for an ill child to find himself addressed in another language. It won't be for long, just until tomorrow morning I imagine, but he needs someone.'

'I'll stay. I'd be glad to.'

'That's fine. A bed will be put up for you by the child's so that you can sleep whilst he is quiet.'

She wondered whether she ought to say that Guy

would be back presently and might want to take her place by his son's bedside, but said nothing, and later, was glad she had not done so. For Guy did not come back to the side ward. Through the long dark night, when Louis had a nightmare and woke terrified, when he ached all over and needed someone to help him take a drink, she dealt with him alone, though on one occasion she did get a night nurse. Of Guy there was no sign. And when, in the early hours, she lay down upon her own bed, she was too tired and too worried about Louis to care what his father might be doing. After all, it was she who loved Louis, she whose instincts had said he was in trouble. And now it was she to whom he clung. The hospital staff might think it odd that the boy's father was content to leave him to the care of his nanny, but what did they matter? Only Louis mattered. Presently, she fell into a fitful doze made hideous by bad dreams in which Renata pushed Louis over the edge of a crater and married Guy in the face of her own furious opposition. She attended the ceremony, miserably unhappy, and was not even amused when she saw that Essie, dressed in a white wig and dog-collar, was taking the service or that Prince Charles, in a primrose taffeta gown with a wreath of roses encircling his huge ears, was the bridesmaid.

So exhausted was she by her disturbed night that she slept straight through the changeover of staff at seven-thirty, and when the day nurse came in and saw the two of them slumbering peacefully, she took pity on them and woke neither.

*   *   *

After a breakfast, which they both slept through, the nurses woke them because the doctor would be doing

129

his rounds, and by a dint of hurrying, Deborah was washed and dressed in time for his visit, though the yellow silk shirt and the wrap-around skirt were not at their best.

'We'll want to do some tests this morning,' the doctor said, when he had examined Louis, who was pale but cheerful now. 'Then we'll get him up for a while, let him try his skill on crutches. In the meantime, Miss Barnett, I suggest you go home, have a shower and a change of clothing and get something to eat. You might have some sleep, too.' The shrewd, tired eyes scanned her countenance. 'I don't suppose you slept for more than an hour or so. If you come back at about three o'clock you can have a cup of tea with him. He'll be properly awake by then, and much more eager for your company.'

'Thank you, doctor. I'd like a wash and change, I must say.' He turned to go and Deborah hesitated to call him back, but she had left her handbag in Guy's car and had not a penny to bless herself with. Should she order a taxi and pay for it when they reached the house, or beg a few coppers from someone and tele-phone Frèremaison to report her plight?

But as the door opened to let the doctor out of the side ward, she saw a figure standing in the corridor, and let out a long breath of relief. Guy! He must have returned to the hospital early to see how Louis was. She moved forward.

'Hello, Guy.'

He came forward and took her hand. The doctor smiled at them both.

'Morning, Monsieur Frenaye. Miss Barnett will tell you that your son's turned the corner, thanks to her, and is now much better.'

'Thanks to me!' Deborah scoffed. 'All I did was sleep in his room! Could you take me back to Frèremaison for a few hours, though? They're going to do some tests and start him walking with crutches, and the doctor suggested that I got some rest and came back around three.'

'Of course.' The hand cupping her elbow pressed slightly. 'You're a good girl. You love Louis, don't you?'

They crossed the hospital foyer and stepped out into the freshness of the morning. Deborah took a deep, luxurious breath.

'Oh, the joys of fresh air instead of air conditioning! Of course I love Louis, he's a very lovable little boy.' She climbed into the car and leaned back against the warm leather seat. 'I feel dirty and untidy and starving hungry, so don't expect much polite conversation on the drive.'

He grinned and took his own place behind the wheel. 'And worn out, I daresay. Never mind, soon have you on your feet again.'

After they had been on the road a few minutes, Deborah felt sufficiently restored to ask a few questions.

'Where did you take Renata, last night? Did she explain what had happened?'

'I took her back to the hotel and stayed with her until she stopped having hysterics.' He shot a wry look at her. 'Yes, she had genuine hysterics, screaming and laughing, the lot. I had to be very firm with her to get her to shut up. Then I gave her a stiff whisky and one of the chambermaids put her to bed. Then I came back to the hospital.'

'Oh, did you?' A glorious glow filled Deborah's mind. So he had not abandoned her for Renata; he had come back!

'Yes, I did. They explained that parents were allowed to stay overnight and I very nearly came and shared your little couch, and then the doctor appeared and spilled the beans that you weren't actually Louis's *maman*.' He grinned at her. 'So of course, after that, they wouldn't let me near you and advised me to go home and get some sleep and be back by ten.'

'I see. But it's not even nine yet!'

'No. Well, I was a bit anxious.'

The warm glow got stronger. Deborah sighed happily. 'I see. Guy, how *did* the accident happen?'

'More or less how we heard. This Raymond boy isn't a bad boy, but he's ten, double Louis's age, and Renata did rather hand over her responsibility, though with the best of motives. She told Raymond that as he was the elder, he was in charge, and of course he was teasing Louis and bossing him about, and when Renata called them to get icecreams, he shouted, "I'm in charge, I'll get there first!" and sort of lunged at Louis. Louis darted backwards, and the rest you know.' He sighed. 'It could have been a good deal worse.'

'It could.' Deborah shuddered. 'It does go to prove, though, that Louis needs other children. I daresay you don't think the local school is quite the thing for your son, but surely when he's so young, it couldn't hurt?'

'The estate school, you mean? I think it's an excellent idea, we'll start him off gradually, with a couple of mornings a week, and you can teach him English in the afternoons.'

'He's getting so good that he won't need lessons soon,' Deborah admitted. 'Before I know it, I'll be *de trop*.'

'As a governess, perhaps.' A quick, wicked glance. 'I'm sure, Miss Barnett, that we can find some other use for you!'

Perhaps fortunately, they drew up in front of the house at this juncture, so Deborah was not called upon to answer the remark but got out of the car and ran towards the front door.

Before she reached it, however, it swung open and Suzanne was there, her face one huge question mark.

'How's Louis? I got breakfast ready, monsieur, like you said.'

'Excellent.' Guy patted Suzanne's shoulder. 'As for Louis, he's well on the road to recovery. I daresay he'll be driving us all mad before the week's out.' He turned to Deborah. 'Upstairs with you, ma petite, and change into something comfortable. Then we'll eat.'

'I'm going,' Deborah said, heading for the stairs. 'And I shan't take long, you can be sure of that!'

*　　*　　*

'Have you had enough? Are you sure, now?'

Deborah lay down her knife and fork with a satisfied sigh. She had devoured everything that had been put in front of her and had downed three cups of milky coffee, but now she was sated.

'Are you being rude about my appetite?' Deborah said suspiciously. 'I couldn't eat another thing. Now I'm going to my room, to sleep and sleep and sleep.'

She rose to her feet and Guy followed suit.

'Good. But why go to your room? If you'd like to try the hammock, I could wake you at lunchtime without having to climb all those tedious stairs.'

'Lunch! I feel as if I shan't have to eat again for a week. But it will be hot in my room with the sun full on the windows.' She eyed the hammock wistfully. Hung between two shade trees it caught the sea breeze and looked very tempting. She turned back to

133

Guy. 'Will you promise not to stare at me whilst I'm asleep?'

He laughed.

'Why on earth should I? If I did, you'd wake up.'

'Ye-es, I might. It's a horrible thought, that some-one could watch you when you're sleeping with your mouth open and your face all unprepared.'

Guy reached across the table and tugged teasingly at a lock of her hair.

'Little goose! What will you do when you marry, wear a mask?'

Deborah laughed and got to her feet. She strolled over to the hammock.

'If I can live with the thought of spending the rest of my life with a man, then I daresay I'll get used to the idea of his seeing my face. But I'm not married to anyone yet, and the thought of being looked at doesn't appeal.' She put out a hand and gently rocked the hammock, then turned to face him. 'How do I get into this thing?'

'Simple, ma belle.' He picked her up as if she weighed no more than a child and stood for a moment holding her in his arms and looking down at her, a mocking smile on his mouth. 'I haven't thanked you, yet, for dragging me off that beach and getting me to the hospital in record time.'

'Oh, that! Do put me down, Guy!'

'Your wish is my command, mademoiselle.' He laid her in the hammock and stood over her, looking down at her, the mocking smile still curving his lips. 'How can I thank you properly?'

She knew what he meant and curled up on her side, a hand beneath her cheek.

'By letting me go to sleep right now, and by being nice to me for a whole week!'

He raised his brows.

'Oho, so you insinuate that I am not always nice to you!' He bent over the hammock and kissed her, very lightly, on the tip of her nose. 'You look like a good little girl lying there — the jeune fille I called you the very first time I set eyes on you. Sweet dreams, chérie.'

* * *

Louis remained in hospital for a week and was much visited before they finally allowed him to go home. He was greeted royally by everyone and spent most of the first day visiting friends on the estate and boasting about his accident.

At first Deborah thought he was unchanged by his experience, apart from a natural desire to show the world how agile he was on his crutches, but soon enough she saw that he was changed.

Louis was curious about his peers. He talked about other patients in the hospital, about the nurses and doctors, and showed great interest in what was happening to his new friends now that he no longer saw them each day.

'Some of the children will be home by now,' Deborah told him. 'But others will be in hospital for a while, yet. Of course, the doctors and nurses work there all the time.' She glanced across at Guy, for they were breakfasting, all three of them, on the terrace. 'I could take you back for a visit if your papa is agreeable?'

'Oh yes, if you please, Papa,' Louis said eagerly. 'Could we go back and see them? And we could go to the animal market, too.'

'A good idea, but not today, mon gars,' his father said. 'Today I've another plan for you. I want Deborah to take you somewhere. How are you

135

managing to get up and down the stairs?'

'He isn't, he gets ignominiously carried,' Deborah admitted. She leaned over and rumpled Louis' hair. 'Shall we go to the hospital tomorrow, then, mon brave?'

'Yes, please! When can Raymond come here?'

Over his head, the two adults exchanged startled glances.

'Raymond?' Deborah did her best to sound soothing. 'He won't come here, pet, don't worry!'

Louis gave her a patronising glance.

'I do not worry. I want to see him! When he came on to the ward I told him about Prince Charles and he said he would like to meet him. Also, he did not see how I can dance on my crutches, or how many famous people have signed my plaster!'

'But I thought . . . '

Guy scraped his chair back and got up to walk round to Deborah and put a calming hand on her shoulder.

'Children are incredible, are they not? I was about to suggest, mademoiselle, that the young man's education might begin this very morning, if you would not object to taking him down to the school.'

Louis looked from one face to the other, his eyes brightening. Deborah cleared her throat. How would his new-found poise react to this one, she wondered.

'Louis, Papa thinks it might be a good idea for you to attend the estate school, for a morning at first, and if you like it, for longer.'

He looked at Deborah, then over to Guy, then back again. His face showed clearly his excitement and uncertainty.

'School? Today?'

'Not if you don't feel like it,' Deborah said quickly.

'But just to see how it goes. I'd be with you, of course.'

Louis nodded, then slid off his chair and picked up his crutches. He swung on to them and began to cross the terrace in long, swinging hops.

'Suzanne, where are you? Today I am to go to school! I shall need pencils, pens, a luncheon box. Quick!'

Deborah waited until he had clattered across the hall and into the kitchen, then she turned to Guy.

'I don't know what to say. I'm speechless! First he wants to see Raymond, then he's thrilled at the idea of school. But it's to be hoped that he likes it because he'll get dreadfully bored, poor scrap, unable to swim or throw a ball for Prince Charles, or to go for walks, play cricket . . . the list of things he can't do is endless, only he hasn't realised it yet.'

'I see what you mean, but we'll try to keep him occupied, between us. You take him down to the school this morning, then I'll take him round the plantation this afternoon. Oddly enough, Renata will still want to take him for outings, she made that clear when she was visiting him the other day, but she said that, for a bit, she'd rather visit him here, with the two of us within call. I think it's a good idea, it'll mean you can have some time to yourself even if he doesn't take to school.'

'Right. I'll take him down there this morning, then.' She hesitated, then glanced up at him. 'Is it far? I wouldn't want him doing his dot and carry one for a long distance.'

They had left the breakfast table and walked across the terrace towards the house as they were talking. Now Guy stopped short.

'Damn! You can't drive, I suppose?'

'I'm afraid not.'

137

'And I'm tied up this morning. Look, I'll give Saunders a ring. He'll run up here in the Land Rover and pick you both up, drop you at the school and fetch you again at lunchtime.'

'Fine, thanks very much.' They stood in the doorway for a moment, looking at each other. Had they thought of everything? It seemed so, for Guy turned away to head across to the front door.

'That seems like it, then. I'll see you both at lunchtime and get a report.'

8

Tom, calling for them as arranged, was required to admire Louis's dexterity with his crutches, his much-autographed plaster, and his school equipment before Louis subsided into the back seat of the Land Rover and became intent upon crayoning his toenails blue, scarlet and yellow with his newly acquired coloured pencils. Deborah glancing back at him, decided to say nothing. It probably meant that Louis was a little more nervous than he would confess!

'Well? How's life?' Tom said, as he turned the Land Rover out of the Frèremaison drive. 'I gather Guy's forgiven Renata for the volcano business.'

'I suppose so. What makes you say it, though?' Deborah enquired. 'I don't know that he ever really blamed her. It could have happened when any of us was with him, if you think about it.'

Tom shrugged. 'Perhaps. He got me to give you a lift because he had a date with the lovely lady, that was what made me remark on it.'

'A date?' Deborah's heart, an unreliable organ of late, promptly sank into her sandals. 'Perhaps they had business to discuss.'

'They did. Guy's thinking of buying a yacht, and Renata wants a hand in the choosing of it.' He shot a quick glance at her. 'Downright sinister, I thought.'

'Why? Surely you don't think he'll . . . ' she glanced behind her, but Louis, head bent, was industriously colouring. ' . . . you don't think he'll *marry* her, do you?'

'I wouldn't like to hazard a guess. When a man's as free with his favours as Guy, it's always difficult to imagine him settling down. But he's done it once, so I suppose he can do it again.' He laughed. 'And Renata *is* Pauline's sister. They may even be twins, for all I know.'

'Yes, but if she ran out on him . . . ' Deborah lowered her voice. 'Surely he'd steer clear of someone who was just like her?'

'Can't tell. Men can be strange over women.' He drew up in the compound before the small school. 'If my laddo starts school, Deborah, what'll you do? Stay on for a bit, go back to England, or look for a job over here?' He looked shyly at her. 'You were a secretary in England, weren't you? You'd have no difficulty in finding a job here. I could help you. We could see more of each other, too, if you were away from Frèremaison.'

Taking Louis into the school, Deborah wondered what Tom had meant when he said they could see more of each other if she were not living at Frèremaison. It seemed a complete contradiction of fact, for with the estate office and the house so near, they could scarcely have been more conveniently situated.

Except, of course, that Guy kept her pretty busy, and that, so far, her outings had been restricted by one thing and another to fairly mild, family treats with Louis in tow.

She shook herself. Foolish, to think about leaving Frèremaison, when it was plain that Louis would need her for a good while yet. Oh, not to teach him

English, perhaps, but to look after him, to love him. Unless, of course, Guy *did* marry Renata. Her heart did its customary dive. And if he did, then there was no way she wanted to stay at Frèremaison, nor on St Lanya. She would go far away, to somewhere where she would not see that dark head, those broad shoulders, the strong, sensitive hands.

'Mademoiselle, what's the teacher's name?'

Louis, burdened with his satchel and his crutches, was making heavy work of the short walk across the school playground. Deborah hastily took his satchel from him and smiled down into his small, enquiring face.

'Miss Lawrence, mon brave.' They reached the door and she held it open for him. 'In we go, and don't forget to be very polite!'

*   *   *

School was to hold one big disappointment for Louis, but in no sense did he dislike it. He watched as children identified letters of the alphabet, painted pictures and learned to do a country dance. He painted a picture of the children's ward at the hospital and wrote, in wobbly capitals, his own name. He drank milk at playtime and sang some songs. In fact, the only disappointment was one which Deborah should have anticipated.

'I'm very sorry, Miss Barnett, but we cannot have Louis here as a pupil whilst he's on crutches, we aren't covered by insurance and the responsibility would be too great,' Miss Lawrence told her visitor regretfully. 'I'm sorry because I agree with you that he's at an age when he needs school, and he's obviously very happy here, but I'm afraid it's out of the question.'

Louis, who had enjoyed every moment of his morning, was dumbfounded to learn that he could not yet become a pupil there.

'Not for *weeks*, Deborah? But I would be so very good!'

When Guy was told, however, he did his best to alleviate the disappointment. He came to meet them instead of Tom, since he said he had finished his business sooner than expected, and picked Louis up, giving him a hug.

'Hola! And how's my schoolboy son?'

Louis promptly burst into tears and Guy held him close, eyeing Deborah over his son's head with horrified bewilderment. What, his glance said, have I done?

'It's all right,' Deborah said quickly. She explained about the teacher's predicament and saw the worry leave Guy's eyes.

He set Louis down again and patted his shoulder.

'Never mind, mon gars, it's only for a while. When the plaster comes off you'll be able to go. Tell you what, I'm not doing anything this afternoon, I'll run you and mademoiselle into town and you can visit your old pals on the ward.'

This did much to reconcile Louis to the situation and by the time they sat down to lunch his normal high spirits had returned, particularly as their first course consisted of steak and kidney pie and chips. Louis's favourite food.

'School was very nice, Papa.' Louis sighed regretfully and stuffed a large chip sideways into his mouth. Guy winced. 'But I will go there soon, and today may I visit the animal market as well as my friends?'

The words were considerably muffled by the insertion of the chip. Guy cast an accusing look at

Deborah. It was she who had insisted that the child share their meals, the look reminded her.

'Don't speak with your mouth full, Louis,' Deborah said automatically. She thought it was right and proper that Louis should have breakfast and lunch with them but she could only join Guy in deploring the child's table manners. However, there was no better way to improve them than to nag him constantly. 'As for school, you'll be spending a good few years of your life there, so don't be in too much of a rush! Tell you what, we'll go to the teashop that Tom took us into that time. And you can have the biggest banana split they sell!'

'OK, mademoiselle.'

Guy stared at Deborah accusingly.

'You are supposed to be teaching my son English, mademoiselle, not slang. Kindly don't teach him to say OK.'

'I didn't. Though I daresay I do say it myself from time to time.' She turned to Louis. 'Who says "OK", mon brave?'

'They say it on telly, mademoiselle. They say it all the time.'

Deborah stared. There was a television set in the house but she had never seen it switched on save in the evenings for the news bulletins.

'The telly? When do you watch telly, Louis?'

'On the ward, mademoiselle. All the good programmes we watched.' He threw his knife and fork down at random on the tablecloth and swung himself over the side of his chair. 'I'm going to see what's for pudding.'

'No, darling!' Deborah said. 'Suzanne will bring it thr — '

Louis, ignoring her, was halfway to the door, crutches swinging.

'Come back here at once!' Guy's voice cracked like a whiplash, but it had the desired effect. Louis turned and swung back to the table, scrambling on to his chair again with great alacrity. Guy sighed. 'And don't you ever get down from the table during a meal again.'

'It's rude, you see, mon brave,' Deborah explained. She rose to her feet. 'I'll just collect the plates and take them to Suzanne, and then Poppy and I will bring in the pudding.'

'Sit down, mademoiselle.' Guy's voice was weary. 'How can I expect the boy to remain seated at mealtimes when you promptly leap to your feet?'

'Oh, but I'm an adult, and I was doing something useful,' Deborah protested, though she sat down quickly enough. 'Gracious, Guy, in normal households one isn't waited on by servants! If I was at home . . . '

'But you are not, mademoiselle. Don't try to make me feel guilty because I have a servant to cook and serve my meals, just enjoy relaxing for once.'

'Well, I don't see . . . ' Deborah was beginning, when Suzanne entered with the pudding, and Poppy came to clear away the first course.

'It's apple pancakes.' Louis announced, peering at the serving dish. 'Apple pancakes, Deborah! *And* with icecream! I bet I finish both mine before you finish one of yours!'

Guy closed his eyes for a moment, his expression one of total suffering.

'Deborah Barnett, what have you done to my life?' he asked as the servants left the room. 'Mealtimes will never be the same again, and I foresee a future plagued with stomach ulcers!'

When the meal was over, Deborah went to her room to change from her neat linen suit into something more comfortable. It would be hot in Castlebridge, and it would also, she felt sure, be an exhausting afternoon, so she intended to take Guy's advice and lie down on her bed for an hour. However, she put on her cool green sundress, did her hair and sprayed perfume at her pulse points before lying down on the bed with a book. She would not fall asleep, but she would read and relax.

She opened her book, found the page, and was asleep before she had read a word.

* * *

She was woken by lips, butterfly soft, touching hers. She stirred sleepily and Louis's voice hissed, 'She's awake!'

It was a shock, to put it mildly, to open her eyes expecting to see Louis's face and find Guy's dark countenance inches from her own. He kissed her once again, lightly, then stepped back, grinning.

'There we are, young master, duty done! Your princess is awake.'

'Duty? What the hell . . . ?' Still half asleep she struggled upright, her cheeks flaming. What a colossal nerve the man had!

'I told him to do it, mademoiselle!' Louis stood close by the bed, beaming down at her. 'Kiss her and she'll wake up like the sleeping beauty did, that's what I said. So Papa did, and you woke just like in the story.'

'So I did.' Deborah pressed her hands to her hot cheeks. 'I never meant to fall asleep and I can't think why I did. I never sleep during the day.'

Guy put out his hands and pulled her to her feet.

'You fell asleep, mademoiselle, because you were exhausted, and no wonder! You've had a very trying week one way and another.'

'Yes, I suppose I have.' She went over to the mirror, grimaced at her reflection, and ran a comb through her hair. Then she picked up her tan shoulder bag, slid her feet into her sandals, and smiled at the two males, watching her expectantly.

'I'm ready. Shall we go?'

During the drive into town, Deborah made a point of sounding Guy out over the possible buying of a pet for Louis. She suggested a bird or perhaps a hamster, and Guy intimated that he was agreeable provided that she and Louis, between them, did all the cleaning, feeding and doctoring of the creature. He dropped them outside the hospital and they spent a happy thirty minutes renewing old acquaintance on the children's ward, where Deborah gleaned the interesting information that, in three weeks' time, Louis would be given a supported heel on the bottom of his plastered foot, so that he might walk without crutches.

'And then you can go to school, so it isn't quite as bad as we'd feared,' Deborah told him.

After the hospital visit, they made their way, by taxi, to the animal market. As they got out of the taxi, Louis was pensive, clutching her hand and staring into the cages as if he expected to recognise one of the occupants.

'I wonder if that puppy will still be here,' he remarked presently, as they neared the tiny shop which had housed his favourite. 'Do you remember him, mademoiselle? The fluffy white one? I loved him best!'

The puppy was still there and the proprietor, remembering Louis from his previous visit, obligingly fetched it out of its wicker cage and put it into the little boy's arms.

146

'Dere! He 'member you well, boy! See how he smile at you?'

Indeed, the puppy did seem delighted to see Louis, wriggling and licking in a transport of affection and accepting an ancient mint and half a crumbling biscuit as if he had not been fed for a month.

'Isn't he lovely, mademoiselle? I wish he was mine more than I wish anything.' Louis glanced sidelong at her. 'Do you suppose, mademoiselle, that someone might buy him for me? After all, I cannot go to school, and I cannot bathe, and it was not *my* fault that I fell into the volcano!' His beseeching eyes were dark with hope. 'Oh, mademoiselle, you did say to Papa might I have a pet, and he would not mind if *you* bought him for me!'

'Yes, but I suggested a hamster, or a lovely parrot in a cage,' Deborah said helplessly. 'Wouldn't you like a parrot, mon brave? You could teach it to talk, and it could ride on your shoulder when you went walking. What do you say? There's a really beautiful blue and red one over there.'

'A parrot couldn't learn to beg, or sleep on my bed at night, or chase a ball, or swim with me when I can swim again,' objected Louis with unanswerable logic. 'Oh, mademoiselle, this little puppy loves me already! He thinks I am his master. He will cry if we put him back in the wicker cage!'

The puppy and Louis eyed her, their expressions so hopeful that it would have taken a heart of stone to deny them.

'Oh, Louis! What makes you think your papa will not be cross if I buy a puppy for you?'

'Because he likes you very much, mademoiselle! Suzanne says so, and Poppy, and even Oliver. And Essie also. They say they hope you won't ever go away, and they say that is how Papa feels, too. Oh

147

mademoiselle, oh, Deb-or-ah, do say I may have this dear little dog!'

The dear little dog turned and licked Louis's nose, then uttered a shrill yap. The proprietor, no doubt sensing a sale, came forward, rubbing his hands.

'Shall I put de little feller back in de cage, missie? Poor feller, him wait long time for someone to love him like dis man love him, but we can't all be lucky, eh? Him brothers and sisters gone, everyone, to good homes and he is lef', so lonely! But p'yaps you come anudder day, eh, boy? Mebbe he not be sole, though dere's a feller wantin' him, a rough type, work dis li'l puppy hard, but a sale's a sale, no good to turn 'way money . . . '

Deborah, seeing Louis's horrified expression, the way he clung to the puppy, stemmed this flood of gentle and probably mendacious eloquence before both she and Louis burst into tears.

'All right, I give in. We'll have the puppy, a collar and a lead. We don't need a basket; all the puppies I know sleep in old grocery boxes lined with blankets; but we'd better have a can of whatever dog food he's been reared on, and a box of puppy biscuits.'

Louis turned to her, his eyes like stars. Above the puppy's soft, fluffy head, his mouth was curved into an enormous smile.

'A dog of my very, very own! My very own dog! Oh, mademoiselle, I love you best in the world!'

*　　*　　*

Burdened with a carrier bag full of little necessities for their new acquisition and with the puppy gambolling at the end of a long, scarlet lead, Deborah still felt lighthearted as they made their way back to the harbour. So the staff at Frèremaison thought Guy

148

liked her very much, did they? She beamed at a passerby and gave a small skip. All nonsense, but still . . . Perhaps it might mean that Renata's grip was losing its strength!

'Mademoiselle, I've been thinking.' Louis did not pause in his steady swing along the pavement but his eyes dwelt thoughtfully on his puppy and then on Deborah's face. 'When we go to the tearoom where we are to meet Papa, it is possible that Prince Edward might do something foolish. Do you think . . . '

'Prince Edward? Who . . . Oh, is that his name?' At Louis's nod, she considered his remark. 'Oh, Lord, you're quite right, of course, it's far too elegant a teashop for the . . . for Prince Edward to feel quite at home. What shall we do?'

They had reached the harbour and Deborah slowed, glancing apprehensively at the teashop, but Louis seemed to have no doubts.

'There's a seat over there, mademoiselle. If I was to sit down on it you could give me Prince Edward, and perhaps you could bring me an icecream outside to eat? I would be very happy to sit on that seat with my puppy whilst you and Papa had some tea.'

'That's a very good idea, but I don't think Papa and I will bother with tea, we'll bring icecreams out too and sit with you. I'll take you across there now, and then wait for Papa in the tearoom. I shan't be long, and I can watch you quite easily.'

'Oh, we'll be all right,' Louis said contentedly, sitting down on the seat and propping his crutches up beside him. 'Can I have Prince Edward now, mademoiselle?'

'Here he is. Bye for now, mon brave.'

Deborah hurried across to the tearoom and went into the cool, dim place, but barely had she arrived

149

before she saw Guy making his way through the big double doors. She went to meet him.

'Where's Louis?' His voice was sharp, and she warmed to the anxiety in it.

'He's outside, watching the goings-on in the harbour. Actually, Guy, he suggested that it might be a good idea if we joined him out there. He'd like an icecream for himself and another for his friend.'

Guy nodded and they went over to the long counter where icecreams were sold to take outside.

'Right. Found a friend already, has he? What sort of ices shall I buy? Chocolate, strawberry, passion fruit — or just plain old vanilla?'

'Louis likes chocolate, and I imagine Prince Edward would like the same.'

'Right.' He turned to the assistant. 'Two chocolate icecreams please, and . . . ' He turned back to stare at Deborah. 'Prince Edward . . . '

'That's right. Could I have a strawberry ice, please? I'm rather hot myself.'

'That's two chocolate icecreams and a strawberry one, please,' Guy said to the assistant. The girl went off and Guy turned to stare, with mounting suspicion, at Deborah. 'You did say Prince Edward, didn't you? I thought Essie's mongrel cur was Prince Charles!'

Deborah took a deep breath and gave Guy her most persuasive smile.

'Essie's dog is Prince Charles, yes. But this . . . this . . . '

Her voice faltered to a stop. Guy had closed his eyes for a moment, then opened them again to stare accusingly at her.

'Don't tell me, you've bought him a dog! And he's on crutches, so he won't be able to exercise it or train it. It'll roam the house at will, chewing up all my clothes, scratching the carpets, biting visitors.' He groaned beneath his breath. 'It didn't occur to you to ask my permission before infesting my house with a mangy flea-ridden cur?'

'Well, it *occurred*,' Deborah, admitted. 'But you know they won't take Louis at school, and the poor lamb does get lonely for other youngsters to play with, and you did say a pet was all right! I suggested a hamster or a parrot and he was *so* disappointed that I agreed to a dog before I'd thought. Anyway, it isn't exactly a dog, it's a tiny puppy.'

The icecreams were delivered and paid for and Guy, holding the two chocolate icecreams, began to walk across to the door.

'Oh, a tiny puppy, well that won't cause *any* trouble,' he said sarcastically. 'Who ever heard of a tiny puppy being a bloody nuisance? Now a full-grown dog can really turn a household upside down, but a puppy . . . '

'Sarcasm,' Deborah said coldly, eating icecream, 'is the lowest form of wit. And don't upset Louis, Guy, his happiness is total. Truly!'

A grunt was her only answer, but when they reached Louis, Guy played up manfully.

'What a splendid little chap,' he declared, hunkering down beside Prince Edward and ruffling the fluffy white head. 'My, and a red collar! He's going to be big, one of these days. What's his name?'

'Prince Edward, we think,' Louis said, presumably using the royal We since he had not consulted Deborah on the subject at all. 'Prince Andrew's nice, but my dog looks more *like* Prince Edward, somehow.'

'Yes, I can see the resemblance,' Guy said, looking doubtfully at the puppy's white fur, quivering little nose and round, dark eyes. 'The question is, how is he going to hold his chocolate icecream? Mademoiselle told me you had a friend with you, so naturally I brought him an icecream as well!'

Louis giggled and began to eat his own ice.

'Papa, if you held it for him, he'd very likely eat it nicely and . . . oh!'

'Problem solved,' Guy remarked, as the icecream vanished in one rapid gulp down the puppy's eager throat. 'No need to ask if he liked it, eh, Louis?'

'I bet he didn't even taste it,' Deborah said teasingly. 'It might just as well have been sawdust the way it went down.'

'He did like it,' Louis protested. 'I could tell, mademoiselle, he really loved it.' He bent over the puppy. 'Didn't you love that icecream, Prince . . . Oh!'

A warning shriek from Deborah came too late. Louis's icecream vanished as rapidly as the puppy's had done. Louis looked ruefully at the empty cone.

'My icecream's gone!'

'My, what lovely manners!' Guy observed sarcastically. 'I suggest that you two and the pup make your way over to the car — see it? — whilst I buy Louis another icecream. You can eat it on the back seat, mon vieux, whilst Deborah and Prince Edward sit in front.'

But this idea did not appeal to Louis at all, and Deborah had to be quite firm with him whilst his father was buying another ice.

'I know you want Prince Edward to sit with you, darling, but if he jumps up and eats another icecream, your papa will really get angry. You want him to like Prince Edward, don't you?'

'Ye-es, but . . .'

'Then do as he tells you and don't make a fuss. The moment the icecream's all eaten up then you shall have the puppy in the back seat with you.'

This promise, however, proved to be easier made than kept. At first, all went according to plan. Guy returned with another chocolate icecream and they got into the car, Deborah in front with Prince Edward on her lap and Louis and the chocolate icecream in the back. But within moments of the car engine purring into life, Prince Edward proceeded to show both fear and disapproval. He lifted his small round face to the heavens, opened his mouth, and proceeded to give what sounded like hoots of dismay, combining this unusual vocal display with lively attempts to escape from Deborah's arms and dive to freedom over the side of the open car.

'Guy, I don't think he feels too good,' Deborah gasped after ten minutes of struggling. 'Guy, I think he's — '

'What now? For God's sake, woman, I'm trying to pass this imbecile without getting us all killed and you begin to chatter! What's wrong *now*?'

'His tummy's heaving,' Deborah said, eyeing her suddenly subdued charge suspiciously. 'And he's dribbling. I think he's going to be . . . Aargh!'

'Poor Prince Edward has been sick,' Louis announced loudly and gratuitously, leaning over Deborah's shoulder. 'Poor puppy, perhaps he could come in the back now. I've finished my icecream.'

Deborah was wearing a cream linen skirt, now awash with secondhand chocolate icecream, and from the way the puppy was behaving, there might well be more to come.

'Oh, this is ghastly! Guy, if you *dare* laugh . . . ' A sideways glance confirmed that he was laughing. 'How can you, when I'm in such a mess? The greedy little beast has ruined my skirt. Oh! Oh, no!'

The second attack, however, removed the grin

from Guy's face most effectively.

'Look at the carpet! It's ruined the carpet, that's for sure. Why did you move, Deborah? The carpet's not something you can just take out and have cleaned, you know, it's part of the car!'

'Why did I move? Monsieur, this skirt cost . . . Anyway, I don't see why . . . '

'Don't let it come over here,' roared Guy, as the puppy showed a desperate desire to exchange the doubtful comforts of Deborah's wet and disgusting skirt for his own immaculate slacks. 'Keep it where it is, for God's sake!' He clutched at his hair. 'Mademoiselle, I *order* you to hold that puppy just where it is!'

Deborah gripped the puppy's furry white tummy firmly and, between giggles, promised not to release it until the car arrived at Frèremaison. Guy perceptibly relaxed.

'Very well. And let us not forget, mademoiselle, who brought this incontinent creature into our lives!'

'Nor who brought him two enormous chocolate icecreams,' Deborah reminded him. 'If he'd not eaten them I'm sure he wouldn't have been sick.'

'Aha! If you'd been honest with me from the start, I wouldn't have bought him an icecream at all. Anyway, it stole the second ice.'

'Oh, Papa, my puppy didn't understand,' Louis announced tearfully from the back seat. 'Don't quarrel, please!'

'I'm not quarrelling with anyone,' Guy said mendaciously. 'Deborah and I are merely . . . '

'Apportioning blame?' Deborah suggested sweetly. 'It's quite all right, mon brave, grownups often get cross over silly things like sticky skirts and carpets. But a good wash will set it all to rights, you'll see.'

154

Guy compressed his lips but, at a murmur from Louis, was forced into at least the appearance of agreement.

'Mademoiselle's right, mon gars, this is nothing that a little soap and water won't mend.' He heard his son's gusty sigh of relief and turned to grin at him. 'It made room for his tea, I suppose.'

9

Suzanne met them at the door with the news that there had been a phone call for Deborah, but that the caller would ring back.

'Thanks, Suzanne. Who was it, or didn't you get the name?'

Suzanne looked guilty.

'I forgot to ask, Deborah. Sorry.'

Father and son had made their way straight to the kitchen quarters to find a suitable grocery box for Prince Edward and Deborah joined them there for a moment.

'Do you need any help? Only I'd like to get out of this skirt and into something a bit more salubrious.'

Guy glanced up at her.

'Sure, go ahead. I'm going out for dinner tonight, so I may not see you again until breakfast time.'

He sounded smug. Deborah smiled brightly, though her heart did one of its predictable dives.

'Oh? Well, it doesn't really matter, since Suzanne and Poppy are both in tonight, and can babysit.' She rumpled Louis's dark hair.

Guy glanced up. His eyes were narrowed and he looked annoyed about something.

'Why should they have to babysit? You didn't mention that you had a date!'

'Nor did you. Anyway, mine isn't a date, exactly.

It's just that I thought I might go and visit Miss Lawrence; she asked me to, and I can always give her a ring.'

'I see.' Guy glanced down at the nest of blankets he was constructing in the grocery box. 'Very well.'

Deborah made her way up to her room, her mind seething with speculation. Yesterday he had been with Renata choosing a yacht, of all things, and tonight, presumably, he was taking her out to dine. Did it mean . . . could it mean, that he was going to ask her to marry him?

She reached her room, stripped, and dived into the shower, emerging ten minutes later clean and sweet smelling, and a good deal soothed. She walked across her room in a tiny white towel just as someone knocked.

'What is it? I'm . . . '

The door opened. Guy stood there. His mouth was grimly set.

'Phone call for you.'

'Oh? Can't you tell whoever it is to ring back?'

'It's Saunders.'

Deborah reached for her towelling robe and pushed her feet into her feathery pink mules.

'Well, would you tell him I'll be right down?'

He left without a word and she slipped into the robe and ran quickly down the stairs. The phone was in the study and so was Guy, glancing idly, it seemed, through some papers. She picked up the receiver.

'Hello, Tom?'

'Hello, Deborah. Any chance of coming out tonight? I happen to know the old man's got a date with Renata, and it's not Suzanne's night off, so I thought we might be lucky for once. Not that it was lucky his answering the phone! He sounded grim.'

Deborah glanced round. Guy was still there,

making no effort to leave her to her conversation. She spoke cautiously, therefore.

'Yes, I know what you mean. And I'd love to come out, Tom. It will be fine, as it happens, because I was going over to see Miss Lawrence this evening, only I'd not got in touch with her, so Suzanne's already agreed to babysit.'

Tom's voice lifted.

'Marvellous! Any idea where you'd like to go?'

She laughed. 'Tom, you must know I haven't got a clue! You choose.'

'Right, put your very best things on, then, and I'll pick you up at eight.'

'I'll be ready. Are you feeding me, or shall I eat first?'

'We'll dine somewhere exotic. Bye, beautiful!'

Deborah put the phone down and turned to meet her employer's baleful gaze.

'So much for Miss Lawrence! I suppose you had this planned all along.'

Deborah was taken aback. His voice was so cold, so sharp.

'Planned? What, going out with Tom, do you mean? Well, as you know, he's tried to take me out half a dozen times this past fortnight, but something's happened to prevent it each time. So tonight seemed a good opportunity.'

Guy snorted.

'Well, don't be taken in by Tom's innocent face. He's not slow in coming forward when he wants something, and you're a pretty girl and a long way from home.'

'I can handle Tom, thank you,' Deborah said crisply. His tone was beginning to annoy her.

'Why not put it off for now, and go somewhere special another night?' Guy said abruptly as she

159

went to pass him in the study doorway. 'I have a very good reason for suggesting it. Tomorrow, for instance, we could make up a foursome.'

She stopped, to stare hard at him.

'With you and Renata, I suppose. No thank you, monsieur, I wouldn't enjoy that at all. I've made my arrangements, and shall keep to them.'

His face was dark. 'Tomorrow, things will be . . . different.' He looked at her and read the answer in her expression. 'Oh, very well, but don't do anything you'll regret!'

And with that he swept out, Deborah thought to herself, going back to her bedroom. What on earth had he been hinting and implying? First, presumably, that Tom was an Unprincipled Beast who would have his way with her and leave her crying. Then, that he was going to do something, tonight, which would change things.

She sighed, then in a mood of defiance got down her newest acquisition. It was the off-the-shoulder dress which consisted of a white satin underslip with a swirl of white chiffon over it, and she had paid less than the price marked on the label because Rosa Dumart had sold it to her cost.

'You will be a very good advertisement for my shop, chérie, wearing that dress,' she had said. 'There is a freshness about you which the dress will accentuate.'

Now, standing before her mirror, Deborah could only agree. Her hair was gleaming like a golden bell, and her figure in the deceptively simple dress looked stunning. What was more she had at last acquired a gentle, golden tan, and she had used just a touch of blue shading on her lids and a new, coral-rose lipstick. The result made her blink then hurry downstairs, hoping to see a gleam in Guy's eyes as he realised what he had missed.

Alas, it was not to be. Guy, Suzanne informed her, had left ten minutes ago, in all the glory of a dinner jacket, for his evening out. But Tom had arrived early and was waiting in the living room.

'Deborah, you look fabulous!' Tom rose to his feet and came towards her, both hands held out. He took her shoulders and kissed her lightly. 'I can't wait to see the way they'll stare, at the Cocoa Tree, when I walk in with you.'

'Where's the Cocoa Tree?' Deborah asked, as they went out to his car. 'I've never heard of it.'

'It's *the* place, where everyone who's anyone goes, sooner or later,' Tom said impressively, handing her into the front seat of his battered old Citroën. 'I just wish I could drive you there in a coach and four, Cinderella.'

'This'll do.' Deborah twinkled across at her escort. 'You look pretty good yourself, I might add!'

Indeed, in a dark suit and white shirt, with his light brown curls brushed flat and his healthily tanned skin glowing with soap and water, Tom did look nice. Wholesome, Deborah thought, and then chided herself. What was wrong with looking wholesome, for goodness sake? It was not given to every man to look dark and dangerous and exciting, like . . .

'Is it far to this place?'

'Not far.' Tom was driving fast but well, and towards the interior of St Lanya rather than towards the coast. 'You'll be impressed, I can guarantee it. I won't tell you any more, though, because I want to see your face when you walk in.'

And the Cocoa Tree certainly lived up to Tom's expectations. Set in groves of palm trees, it was built in white stone like a fairy palace, around the edge of three or four natural lakes. They arrived in darkness, but the place was lit by a myriad of coloured lights, cunningly concealed in the trees, reflecting out of the lakes, so that Deborah's involutary gasp was all that Tom could have wished.

'It's beautiful, Tom.' She took his hand and they wandered down a path beside the largest of the lakes which led to one of the arched openings, through which they could see golden candlelight and hear soft music. 'Gracious, what a huge dance floor! Oh, and the flowers!'

Inside the arches, flowers were banked in colourful profusion and the small tables set round the shining, golden parquet of the dance floor were set with pale yellow tablecloths and had a gold vase in the centre of each with a selection of flowers ranging from palest cream to deepest amber.

'Impressive, isn't it?' Tom said with satisfaction as the head waiter ushered them to a table. 'Sometimes they do the tables and the flowers in pink, but I prefer them in gold.' They sat down and took the huge menus. 'Glance around you, Deborah, and see if you recognise celebrities. There's Sandra Welsh, with her third husband, or is he her fourth? And that fellow that plays the trumpet so marvellously — Acker Bilk. And a bit further round . . . '

' . . . are Guy and Renata,' Deborah said in a hollow voice. 'Oh, Tom, shall we leave?'

Tom leaned across the table and took her hand.

'Don't be an idiot, Deb, a cat can look at a king! Anyway, I wanted to talk to you about Guy and now's as good a time as any.'

'What, with him sitting there? Tom, do let's go somewhere else!'

The waiter, arriving with their seafood starters, banished all thoughts of flight, however. Not only was the food delicious, but Deborah knew that she could not run away, nor had she any right to ruin Tom's evening. So she ordered her meal and, whilst they waited for it to arrive, consented to dance.

'He's spotted us,' Tom breathed in her ear as they circled the floor in each other's arms. 'He's staring as if he can't believe his eyes. He doesn't look very pleased.' He gave her a squeeze. 'Our boss, Debbie, is a dog-in-the-manger.'

'I know,' Deborah admitted. 'Oh, look, our first course has arrived. Shall we go back?'

Over the best charcoal grilled steak she had ever tasted, Tom told her a bit more about Guy.

'I expect you know that he married Renata's sister Pauline because she was pregnant,' he announced cheerfully through a mouthful of jacket potato. 'She was a promising young actress in Paris at the time and seemed to be madly in love with him. He brought her here to have the baby, because she said she didn't want to be seen by the people who mattered when she looked at her worst.'

'I see. And then?'

'Oh, then she had the baby and when Louis was four weeks old she ran off with Toby Kristensen, the bandleader, leaving the child behind. Guy divorced her and never mentioned her name again, so they say. It gave him a jaundiced view of women, though, to put it no stronger. He takes what he wants from them and gives nothing in return, and you can understand why. Only . . . ' He hesitated, glancing diffidently across the table at her.

'Go on, don't mind my feelings,' Deborah said. reassuringly.

'Only he's terribly attractive, and I don't want to see you hurt. There was a nice kid who worked at Frèremaison once, Ada her name was. It was about three years ago, and perhaps the wound of the way Pauline had treated him was still raw, but . . . well, to put it bluntly he had a glorious and very obvious affair with Ada in full view of the whole island and then, when she must have made it plain that she expected marriage, he packed her off home to England.'

'Very wise,' Deborah said, though her hands felt clammy. 'Heartless, perhaps, but if he didn't love her . . .'

'I'm sure he never pretended to love her. But she was absolutely heartbroken, she'd been so *sure* . . .' He took her hand beneath the table. 'Deborah, I couldn't bear it to happen to you!'

'It won't. I promise you.'

Tom fetched a deep sigh. 'I believe you. Shall we dance again when you've chosen a pudding?'

*   *   *

'Will you come in for coffee, Tom? Suzanne's still up, and she's always marvellous about leaving coffee and sandwiches out for anyone who's been gadding.'

Tom smiled and linked fingers.

'Yes, please, if the boss man won't object.' They entered the hall, blinking in the bright light. 'I wonder if he's home yet?'

Deborah, who had suffered the agony of seeing Guy dancing with Renata, laughing with her, bending solicitously over her as he handed her into the car, sniffed.

'No, he'll be hours yet. He's got to dance attendance on Renata, get her back to her hotel, and so on. You sit in the living room and I'll go and get the coffee.'

But Suzanne, very ready for bed, nevertheless

insisted on making the coffee before she plodded upstairs.

'Goodnight, both,' she called as she crossed the lower hall. 'If you want food, it's under the white tablecloth in the kitchen.'

'If we want food, after that spread! Never again, I shouldn't think! Well, not until breakfast time anyway.' Deborah sank on to the sofa beside Tom and put her coffee cup on the occasional table nearest her. 'Thanks, Tom, for an unforgettable evening!'

'It was nice, wasn't it, darling Deb? Let's make it perfect!'

He kissed her nicely, his lips firm, his hands staying decorously on her bare shoulders. He was deepening the kiss, his hands beginning to smooth down her back, when a voice broke across his tentative lovemaking.

'What the devil . . . ?'

Shock sent them flying to opposite ends of the sofa, hearts pounding. Deborah glared up at Guy as coldly as she knew how.

'I'm sorry, monsieur, we didn't hear you come in.'

'So I gather!' And what do you think you were doing?'

'Saying goodnight in the usual fashion,' Tom said coolly. He had moved back towards Deborah, and now he put a defensive arm round her shoulders. 'I'm not accustomed to being bawled at just for kissing a girl!'

'Aren't you indeed! Then, since you've said goodnight, you'd better go home and then you won't be bawled at. Or punched on the nose, either.'

Tom got to his feet. Deborah could see that he was trying very hard to keep his temper.

'Deborah's old enough to choose who she kisses, monsieur, and that's all I was doing — kissing her!'

Deborah, who had also risen, put a restraining hand on his arm.

'It's all right, Tom, I'll come and see you off.' She turned to Guy. 'Look, I invited Tom in for coffee and then we sat on the sofa, drank it and kissed, as I would have done without a qualm in my own home. If you don't think that's what I should do, I'd better take Tom up to my bedroom next time he takes me out!'

For a moment an expression of such naked fury crossed his face that she flinched back, then it was gone and his face was cold once more. But Tom had seen it to. He put his arm round her.

'Come back to my place, Deborah. You can sleep in my spare room and come back here tomorrow to sort things out with Monsieur Frenaye.'

Deborah shook her head, then stood on tiptoe and kissed Tom's cheek.

'It's all right. Monsieur Frenaye's quite civilised when he isn't in a rage. We'll sort it out as soon as you've gone.' She went to the front door with Tom, adding, sotto voce, 'I shall go straight up to bed and I'll lock my door, so don't worry, Tom.'

She stood in the doorway until Tom's Citroën had disappeared down the drive, then turned reluctantly back indoors. Guy had behaved like the very worst sort of Victorian father, not like a man whose own behaviour where women were concerned was a good deal less than perfect. He stood at the foot of the stairs now, his face stern.

'Come into the living room please, Deborah. I want to talk to you.'

'And I want to go to bed,' Deborah said defiantly, but with a thumping heart. 'We can talk in the morning. Goodnight, monsieur.'

She went to pass him and he caught her by the

shoulders, swinging her round to face him. His eyes smouldered down into hers.

'You said goodnight to Tom Saunders in a much friendlier fashion.'

She stiffened indignantly, trying to jerk herself free.

'Tom hadn't just insulted me. Let me go!'

'Why should I? You ruined my evening, you know. Cuddling up to Saunders, talking, laughing . . . I couldn't concentrate on what I was doing, all I could do was watch the pair of you and wonder whether he was going to succeed where I'd failed.'

It was too much. Deborah wrenched herself out of his grasp and ran up the stairs. Safe on the upper landing, with Guy still standing in the hallway, she leaned over the banisters and addressed him.

'How dare you insult Tom by insinuating that he'd treat me the way you did! He's a decent, hard-working young man, not a spoilt playboy who thinks women were put on the earth for his enjoyment, to pick up and throw down as he wishes! As for kissing you goodnight, why the hell should I? Go and get Renata to kiss you, if you're desperate for affection!'

She saw him start to mount the stairs two at a time and fled, slamming her bedroom door shut and shooting the bolt across. He banged on the panels.

'Deborah! Come out!'

'No. Go away, Guy, go back to Renata. I never want to see you again as long as I live!' She was crying, tension and misery combining to break down the barriers she had raised against her own feelings for him. She loved him, of course she did, but he would never know and nor would anyone else!

'Deborah! Are you going to come out or not?'

'I s-said no and I m-meant no!'

Even through the door panel, she could hear the

change in his voice.

'Deborah? Oh, my God!'

She was still leaning against the locked door, weeping silently, when he came through from Louis's room and took her in his arms. Too shocked to resist with much force, she sagged against his chest and sniffled into his white dinner jacket.

'Go away,' she said, between sniffles, in a voice which totally lacked conviction. 'I know all about you, Guy Frenaye. You m-make love to girls until they're crazy about you and then you move on to the next one. I won't be just another conquest on your list! Particularly now, when it's obvious that you're going to be married.'

'True.' He kissed the top of her head, which was all he could get at, then tilted her chin so that her tear-drowned eyes were looking into his. 'That's why I took Renata out to dinner.'

'I know. Well, I wish you happiness.' But she did not move from the comfort of his arms.

'Deborah, be honest!'

'Very well!' She blinked the tears away and sniffed again. 'I hope you'll be very miserable. You deserve to be!'

'In fact, I think I'm going to be very happy. I told Renata, this evening, that I was getting married, and asked her if she'd take care of Louis whilst we honeymooned around the islands. She was very annoyed and refused pointblank, so I suppose we'll have to get Essie to do it.'

'If you aren't marrying Renata . . . ' coloured lights exploded in Deborah's mind. There must be another explanation, of course, but for the life of her she could not think of it!

'I want to marry you, ma belle!' He kissed the tears from her cheeks. 'You've led me such a dance, but I

168

knew it would be you and no one else right from that night when Louis thought I was eating you. Now will you kiss me?'

It was a satisfactory kiss, but he broke it far too soon for Deborah, who uttered a little mutter of protest and cuddled closer against him. Then she looked up at him, her eyes bright.

'Do you love me, Guy? I've loved you for ages and ages, only I knew what you were like, so I kept smacking all my urges on the head. Why do you want to marry me?'

He picked her up and carried her over to the bed, then sat down with her on his knee.

'One question at a time, if you please, mademoiselle! I love you, which is a damned good reason for wanting to marry you. The other reason is that it's the only way of getting you!'

Deborah smiled.

'When you sneaked in through Louis's door just now, and put your arms round me, something clicked in my head. Or my heart, I'm not sure which.' She looked up at him, her blue eyes candid. 'I might have put up a token struggle, but I'd made up my mind to be overpowered!'

'Now she tells me, after I've committed myself!' He paused, to kiss her again. 'But I wouldn't have allowed you to seduce me, ma chérie, because I want you for always, not just until you choose to move on.'

'I see. All you want is an unpaid nanny for Louis! Well, I'll think about it and let you know.'

'You'll give me your word that you'll marry me here and now, or . . . ' a significant glance at the bed on which they sat made her laugh and kiss his chin.

'You know very well I want to marry you more than . . . oh, more than anything! Now, monsieur, you've got some explaining to do. Why did you take

Renata hunting for a yacht? Why did you suggest a foursome tomorrow night? And that's only the start!'

'I took Renata round a yacht I'd already bought, because she wanted to see it,' he corrected. 'I want the yacht for our honeymoon, of course. And I suggested a foursome tomorrow night because I didn't want you seeing Saunders tonight. I knew he was serious about you, he'd more or less told me so, and I was deathly afraid he'd ask you before I'd come clean with Renata. I *had* led her to believe she interested me more than a little, I blush to confess.'

'Was she your mistress, Guy?'

He slid her off his knee and stood up, looking down at her, his eyes gleaming beneath lowered lids.

'That, chérie, is neither here nor there. Come down to the study and we'll have a drink to celebrate our engagement.'

'She was. I thought as much.' Deborah nodded to herself. 'Are we engaged now, then?'

'Of course. I proposed and you accepted. Come along.' He unlocked her door and they went quietly through the moonlit house and down into the study, where Guy picked up a decanter and two glasses and took them through to the living room. He sat down on the couch without putting the light on and patted the cushion beside him. Deborah sat down and took the drink he poured, then began to sip it. Presently, when they had toasted each other, he turned to her and took her in his arms.

'Guy, I thought you said you wouldn't . . . '

'I know I did. After what happened last time I tried to seduce you in your bedroom, are you surprised?' His hands slid across her back, then strong fingers pushed up into the hair at the nape of her neck. 'Oh my God, chérie, I want you so badly!'

'So you did try to seduce me,' Deborah said

dreamily, as he moved over her and began to kiss her throat. 'I often wondered what would have happened if Louis hadn't walked in.'

'Stop talking,' a muffled voice ordered, 'and you may well find out!'

They were completely absorbed in the first tentative and beautiful stage of making love when the door opened and the light clicked on. They shot apart, Deborah breathing a sigh of relief that the interruption had come whilst they were both still fully clothed and capable of rational thought, even as it occurred to her that it might be burglars.

It was not burglars. Louis, in his sleeping suit, stood in the doorway, his arms full of puppy.

'He was crying and crying, mademoiselle,' he complained. 'So I came downstairs to fetch him, because I couldn't sleep when my poor Prince Edward was so unhappy. He was standing right outside this door,' he continued, fixing them with an accusing stare. 'Yes, right outside here, crying and crying, and you never heard a thing!'

The End